Crazy
Cock

OTHER WORKS BY HENRY MILLER PUBLISHED BY
GROVE WEIDENFELD:

Black Spring
Quiet Days in Clichy
Sexus
Plexus
Nexus
Tropic of Cancer
Tropic of Capricorn
Under the Roofs of Paris

Crazy Cock

Henry Miller

FOREWORD BY ERICA JONG

INTRODUCTION BY MARY V. DEARBORN

GROVE WEIDENFELD
New York

Published by Grove Weidenfeld
A division of Grove Press, Inc.
841 Broadway
New York, NY 10003-4793

Henry Miller: *Letters to Emil*. Copyright © 1968 by Henry Miller.
Reprinted by permission of New Directions Publishing Corporation.

Library of Congress Cataloging-in-Publication Data

Miller, Henry, 1891–1980
Crazy cock / Henry Miller. — 1st ed.
p.   cm.
ISBN 0-8021-1412-1 (alk. paper)
I. Title.
PS3525.I5454C7   1991
813'.52—dc20   91-9247
                                                    CIP

Manufactured in the United States of America

Printed on acid-free paper

Designed by Irving Perkins Associates

First Edition 1991

1   3   5   7   9   10   8   6   4   2

Foreword

CERTAIN WRITERS become protagonists. Their writings and their biographies mingle to create a larger myth, a myth which exemplifies some human tendency. They become heroes. Or antiheroes. Byron was one such writer. Pushkin, another. Colette exemplified a kind of female heroism. As did George Sand. And de Beauvoir.

Miller is the only American who stands in their company, and appropriately enough, he is more honored in France than in his own country. His writing is full of imperfection, bombast, humbug. But the purity of his example, his heart, his openness, will, I believe, draw new generations of readers to him. In an age of cynicism, he remains the romantic, exemplifying the possibility of optimism in a fallen world, of happy poverty in a world that worships Lucre, of the sort of gaiety Yeats meant when he wrote "their ancient, glittering eyes are gay."

I knew Henry Miller. In a number of ways, he was my mentor. I was a very young writer, very green and suddenly famous, and he, a very old writer, seasoned in both fame and rejection, when we met—by letter—and became pen pals, then pals. I feel lucky to have known him, and in some sense, I feel that I only got to know him well after his death.

Miller was the most contradictory of characters: a mystic who was known for his sexual writings, a romantic who pretended to be a rake; he was above all a writer of what the poet Karl Shapiro called "wisdom literature." If we have trouble categorizing Miller's "novels" and consequently underrate and misunderstand them, it is because we judge them according to some unspoken notion of "the well-wrought novel." And Miller's novels seem not wrought at all. In fact, they are rants—undisciplined and wild. But they are full of wisdom, and they have that "eternal and irrepressible freshness" which Ezra Pound called the mark of the true classic.

In the profound shocks and upheavals of the twentieth century—from the trenches of World War I to Auschwitz to the holes in the ozone layer—we in the West have produced a great body of "wisdom literature," as if we needed all the wisdom we could get to bear what may be the last century of humans on earth. Solzhenitsyn, Günter Grass, Neruda, Idries Shah, Krishnamurthi, Sartre, de Beauvoir all write predominantly wisdom literature. Even among our most interesting novelists—Bellow, Singer, Lessing, Yourcenar—the fictional form is often a cloak for philosophical truths about the human race and where it is heading. The popularity of writers like Margaret Mead and Joseph Campbell in our time also serves to show the great hunger for wisdom. We are, as Ursula Le Guin says, "dancing at the edge of the world," and it takes all our philosophy to bear it.

Henry Miller did not come to his profession easily. He was over forty before he had his first book published (*Tropic of Cancer*), and by then he had won the reputation of a bum and a no-good in the eyes of his very bourgeois German-American family.

He had been struggling for years to find his voice as a writer, and *Crazy Cock* is interesting principally for the way it recounts that struggle. Put beside *Tropic of Cancer* it is almost a textbook study of a writer looking for a voice.

The voice of Miller in *Crazy Cock* is third person, stilted, fusty. Henry appears to be ventriloquizing a Literary Voice—with a capital "L."

The writer who *invented* first person, present tense exuberance for the twentieth century is writing here in the third person! And it doesn't suit him. It makes him use words like "wondrous," "totteringly," "blabberingly," "fragrant," and "abashed." Here is Henry the Victorian, the reader of Marie Corelli, writing in a pastiche of Victorian romance and Dreiserian realism. Blabberingly indeed!

But *Crazy Cock* is fascinating for what it tells us about Miller's literary roots. Henry Miller was born an heir to the Victorian age—(even in the seventies, when I knew him, he used to rave to me about Marie Corelli)—and *Crazy Cock* shows us what Henry had to overcome to find his own voice as a writer.

Here is the voice of Henry Miller in *Crazy Cock*.

She was more beautiful than ever now. Like a mask long withheld. Mask or mask of a mask? Fragments that raced through his mind while he arranged harmoniously the inharmony of her being. Suddenly he saw that she was looking at him, peering at him from behind the mask. A rapport such as the living establish with the dying. She rose, and like a queen advancing to her throne, she approached him. His limbs were quaking, he was engulfed by a wave of gratitude and abasement. He wanted to fling himself on his knees and thank her blabberingly for deigning to notice him.

Now listen to the sound of *Tropic of Cancer*.

I have no money, no resources, no hopes. I am the happiest man alive. A year ago, six months ago, I thought that I was an artist. I no longer think about it, I *am*. Everything that was literature has fallen from me. There are no more books to be written, thank God.

This then? This is not a book. This is libel, slander, defamation of character. This is not a book, in the ordinary sense of the word. No, this is a prolonged insult, a gob of spit in the face of Art, a kick in the pants to God, Man, Destiny, Time, Love, Beauty . . . what you will. I am going to sing for you, a little off key perhaps, but I will sing. . . .

Henry is retracing his steps as an artist here, telling us exactly what happened between *Moloch* and *Crazy Cock*, and *Tropic of Cancer*: he let go of literature. It reminds me of Colette's advice to the young Georges Simenon: "Now go and take out the poetry."

Good advice. A writer is born at the moment when his true voice of authority merges at a white heat with the subject he was *born* to chronicle. Literature falls away and what remains is *life*—raw, pulsating life: "a gob of spit in the face of Art."

For the truth is that every generation, every writer, must rediscover *nature*. Literary conventions tend to ossify over time, and what was once new becomes old. It takes a brave new voice to rediscover real life buried under decades of literary dust. In unburying himself, Henry unburied American literature.

The style of writing Henry Miller discovered has itself become convention, so it is hard to grasp how electric it seemed in 1934. The feminist critique of the sixties came in to bury Henry under rhetoric—just as false, in its way, as the rhetoric of male supremacy. But the feminist critique neglects to ask the main question Henry Miller poses: *How does a writer raise a voice?* The problem of finding a voice is essential for *all* writers but is more fraught with external difficulties for women writers because no one agrees what the proper voice of woman is—unless it is to keep silent. This, by the way, accounts for all the trouble feminists, including me, have with Henry. He liberates himself, becomes the vagabond, the clown, the poet, but the open road he chooses is *never* open to the other sex. Nevertheless, it is useful to trace the steps of his liberation: Paris plus first person bravado equals the voice we have come to know as Henry Miller.

Henry found this voice primarily in his letters to Emil Schnellock, his pal from the old neighborhood (who lent him the $10 that was in his pocket when he sailed to Europe in 1930 and with whom he left the manuscripts of *Crazy Cock* and *Moloch* for safekeeping*). Henry's *Letters to Emil* constitutes an amazing record of a writer finding his voice. The transition from the tortured prose of *Crazy Cock* to the explosive simplicity of *Tropic of Cancer* is all there. We hear the explosion as writer finds his sound. We see the contrail streaked across the sky.

Editor's note: There is some debate over who took possession of *Crazy Cock* and *Moloch* once Henry Miller left for Paris. For a different interpretation see Mary Dearborn's introduction, page xv.

Henry Miller's writing odyssey is an object lesson for anyone who wants to learn to be a writer. How do you go from self-consciousness to unself-consciousness? *Crazy Cock* will show you the first part of the journey. *Tropic of Cancer* is the destination.

In between come his *Letters to Emil*. These letters are crucial because they are written to someone who accepts him completely and with whom he can be wholly himself. In them, he practices the voice that will revolutionize the world in *Tropic of Cancer*. It is the voice of the New York writer revolting against New York. And it is the voice of the weary picaro—weary of flopping from pillar to post.

> Two years of vagabondage has taken a lot out of me. Given me a lot, too, but I need a little peace now, a little security in which to work. In fact, I ought to stop living for a long while, and just work. I'm sick of gathering experiences.
>
> There'll be a lot to tell when I get back to New York. Enough for many a wintry night. But immediately I think of N.Y. I get frightened. I hate the thought of seeing that grim skyline, the crowds, the sad Jewish faces, the automats, the dollars so hard to get, the swell cars, the beautiful clothes, the efficient businessmen, the doll faces, the cheap movies, the hullabaloo, the grind, the noise, the dirt, the vacuity and sterility, the death of everything sensitive. . . . (to Emil from The Dôme, Paris, October 1931)

The total acceptance that Emil provided made possible the voice of the *Tropic*s. The perfect audience for any writer is, in fact, an audience of one. All you need is one reader who *cares*, and cares uncritically. It is no wonder that Nabokov dedicated nearly every book to his wife, Vera. And no wonder that, in my perplexity about newfound fame, the madness of the movie business, my dilemma about how to write a second novel, I turned to Henry Miller in 1974. He was willing to be a generous sounding board for me as Emil Schnellock had been for him. He passed the gift of uncritical acceptance along. In a world where writers take virtually every opportunity to trash one another, Henry Miller was a wonder of generosity.

I think he was willing to be that for me because his own road as a writer had been so very hard to travel. He had to pull up roots, go to Paris, live like a clochard in order to find the freedom to be an artist.

Brassai records the transformation that came over Miller in Paris: "In France, his brow smoothed out, he became happy, smiling. An irrepressible optimism irradiated his whole being."

The New York that Henry left in March of 1930 was nowhere as fraught as the New York of today, but it still bore certain similarities. In New York it was a dishonor to be an unknown writer; in Paris one could write *écrivain* on one's passport and hold one's head high. In Paris it was *assumed* (it still is today) that an author had to have time, leisure, talk, solitude, stimulation. In New York it was, and still is, assumed that unless you fill up your time with appointments, you are a bum.

More than that (and more important, particularly for Henry) was the American attitude toward the vagabond artist—an attitude which unfortunately persists to our day. "In Europe," as Brassai says in his book *Henry Miller: Grandeur Nature*, "poverty is only bad luck, a minor unhappiness; in the United States it represents a moral fault, a dishonor that society cannot pardon."

To be a poor artist in America is thus *doubly* unforgivable. To be an artist in America is anyway to be a criminal (its criminality pardoned only by writing best-sellers, or selling one's paintings at usurious rates to rich collectors and thus feeding the war-machine with tax-blood). But to be poor *and* an artist—this is un-American.

Which of us has not felt this disapproval, this American rejection of the dreamer? "Poets have to dream," says Saul Bellow, "and dreaming in America is no cinch."

In the last few years we have seen a dramatic replay of these attitudes in the debates over censorship and the National Endowment for the Arts. Our essential mistrust of the dreamer leads us to cripple him or her with restrictions of all sorts. We seem not to understand that the basic wealth of our country—wealth and emotional health—comes from our creative spirit. Even with Japanese conglomerates buying our movie companies, even with statistics that prove that our movies, music, television shows, and inventions are our biggest exports in real dollar terms, we still honor the money-counters and money-changers above the inventors and dreamers, who give them something to count and change.

This is a deep-seated American obsession, and one whose historical genesis it would be fascinating to retrace. It comes, of course, out of puritanism and its assumption that dream-life and imagination are suspect. We must understand how Henry was buffeted about by these forces and how he fled to Europe to be reborn. As Brassaï says, "It was the scorn which ultimately Miller could not stand. It was the scorn that he wanted to escape. Madness and suicide threatened him." Miller himself writes in *Tropic of Capricorn*, "Nowhere have I known such a degradation, such a humiliation as I have known in America."

Crazy Cock is fascinating because it shows us the New York that Miller fled and the reasons that he had to flee in order to find himself as a writer. Just as the Paris books are bursting with sunshine, *Crazy Cock* is dour, dismal, gray. The liveliest thing about it is its title.

Still, it is a vital part of the Miller canon. It shows us how far he had to travel to become the Henry Miller who breathed fresh air into American literature.

—ERICA JONG
May 1991

Introduction

THE YEAR WAS 1927. Henry Miller's second wife had just run away to Europe with her Lesbian lover. He was recovering from an extended period of what he called nervous disintegration. Penniless and humiliated, he had been forced to move back in with his parents, who were dismayed at their thirty-six-year-old son's failure to live up to their eminently bourgeois expectations. In desperation, he had taken a dead-end office job offered him by a childhood rival. One evening, however, he stayed after work and began typing without pause. After midnight, a sheaf of closely typed pages—a torrent of words—lay next to his typewriter. They were notes for the book Miller felt he was destined to write: the story of his marriage to June, her love for Jean Kronski, and his utter debasement in the face of this betrayal. The notes would become *Crazy Cock*, Henry Miller's third novel and his surest move toward *Tropic of Cancer*, the literary accomplishment that would follow just a few years later.

This was not Miller's first attempt at writing. He had always expected that he would become a writer, or something equally exceptional. For Miller, even his very birthdate, one day after Christmas in 1891, suggested his specialness;

he later stated it was a year of extraordinary literary significance.

Born to middle-class German-American parents—his father was a tailor—Henry was precocious, and the family had high expectations for his future. As an adolescent, however, he came to scorn traditional schooling and became a confirmed autodidact. Family circumstances ruled out college, except for a brief stint at tuition-free City College, and instead Henry reluctantly joined his father in his tailor shop in 1913. He made his first serious attempt at writing—an essay on Nietzsche—at this time, but he did his most important work on his walks to and from the tailor shop; he later said that he wrote whole enormous volumes in his head, tomes about his family's history and his own boyhood, and indeed traces of these early "works" made their way into later books such as *Black Spring* and *Tropic of Capricorn*.

In 1917 he married and soon fathered a child. Faced with these responsibilities, he took a job as an employment manager at Western Union, the Cosmodemonic Telegraph Company of his later books. He had to hire and fire messengers, and the turnover was incredible; the absurdity of the job reduced him to despair. On a three-week vacation in 1922, he willed into being a book-length manuscript. Galled by his employer's suggestion that it was too bad there was no Horatio Alger tale about a messenger, and inspired by the example of Theodore Dreiser's *Twelve Men*, which he much admired, Miller turned out a work he would call *Clipped Wings*. The title referred to the wings on the Western Union symbol, and the book was a portrait of twelve messengers, angels whose wings had been clipped. The fragments of the manuscript that survive indicate that the book was a tedious exercise in cynicism and misanthropy; Miller himself said that he knew it was "faulty from start to finish . . . inadequate, bad, *terrible.*"

He returned to Western Union, passive and pessimistic, less certain than ever of his writing future, trapped in a loveless marriage. Then, on a chance visit to a Times Square dance hall, he met June Mansfield Smith, the Mona of *Tropic of Cancer*, the Hildred of *Crazy Cock*, the Mara of *The Rosy Crucifixion*, the mythified "her" to whom *Tropic of Capricorn* is dedicated. Mysterious, dramatic, spellbindingly beautiful, June won Henry immediately. He was mesmerized by her torrential talk, her spinning of intricate and shadowy tales involving intrigues with other men; in *Crazy Cock* he would describe her as "a veritable honeycomb of dissimulations." June surrounded herself with chaos, and Miller thrived on it. He later wrote in *Tropic of Capricorn*:

> I thought, when I came upon her, that I was seizing hold of life. . . . Instead I lost hold of life completely. I reached out for something to attach myself to—and I found nothing. But in reaching out, in the effort to grasp, to attach myself, left high and dry as I was, I nevertheless found something I had not looked for—*myself.*

Most important, he learned that what he wanted was "not to live—if what others are doing is called living—but to express myself." For June insisted, unconditionally, that he throw over his Western Union job (and his wife and child) in order to write. Just months after they were married in June 1924, Henry began his writing life. June supported them through a succession of hostessing jobs in the Village and, increasingly, with money brought in by elaborate schemes involving her numerous admirers—an activity she called "gold digging," but which seems actually to have been a kind of genteel prostitution.

Miller later said he was so in love with the idea of becoming a writer that he could not write. With uncharacteristic humility, he began by trying to get magazine assignments. He warmed up by writing a series of small sketches, meditations on such subjects as Brooklyn's Navy Yard and wrestling heroes, and submitting them feverishly to popular magazines—which almost invariably rejected them. June and he hatched a plan to print these sketches on colored pieces of cardboard and to sell them door to door. Before long, June integrated the "Mezzotints," as they called these broadsides, into her confidence games; her admirers would buy whole runs of prose poems in exchange for her company—or, more likely, her sexual favors. She managed to get one published in a magazine called *Pearson's*, but it appeared under her name, not Henry's. His writing became currency in her sexual transactions, with results for his development as a writer that were, predictably enough, not salutary. His work was flat, uninspired, laden with detail, and couched in baroque language.

Miller's second novel, written in 1928, was a product of this compromised set of circumstances. As part of an elaborate seduction of a wealthy old man she identified only as "Pop," June appropriated Henry's efforts as her own, turning to Pop for support for a novel *she* was writing. He agreed to give her a weekly stipend if she showed him some pages each week—pages that would be written by her husband. In these constrained circumstances Miller turned out *Moloch, or This*

Gentile World, an autobiographical portrait of Dion Moloch, a Western Union man married to a nagging and prudish woman. Another "arrangement," however, was to have an even greater impact upon his writing during this period.

Moloch was written when Miller was in recovery after the complete breakdown caused by June's love affair with Jean Kronski. In 1927 the two women left for Paris, and in June's absence Henry began describing the events that led to his breakdown, collecting notes that would shape *Crazy Cock* and, later, *Tropic of Capricorn* and *The Rosy Crucifixion*. As his first attempt to transmute those galvanizing experiences into art, *Crazy Cock* is a riveting document indeed.

The story he had to tell was almost nightmarish. While Henry tried to write in the Millers' Brooklyn Heights apartment, June worked at a variety of hostessing and waitressing jobs in Greenwich Village. As part of the Village's bohemian subculture, June came into contact with all kinds of conspicuous characters, from slumming millionaires to androgynous doyennes of the night. One such character, who was to become the Vanya of *Crazy Cock*, appeared one day in the restaurant where June worked, newly arrived in town from the West Coast and looking for work. June thought her extraordinarily beautiful: she had long black hair, high cheekbones, violet eyes, and a confident walk. She wanted to be an artist, the woman said, and she showed June a puppet she called Count Bruga, a garish and frightening affair, which June propped up against the headboard of her marital bed. June renamed her Jean Kronski, inventing for her a romantic past that included descent from the Romanoffs.

June and Jean quickly became inseparable, Jean moving to Brooklyn to be closer to June. Henry soon realized that

Mary V. Dearborn

Jean was a major contender for June's affection. He became obsessed with determining the exact nature of their attachment. He was sure Jean was a Lesbian, but was June? Preoccupied throughout his early life with questions of sexual identity, Miller now saw his hard-won sense of manhood entirely undone by June's violent attraction to another woman. His working notes for *Crazy Cock* read at this point: "Commence to go really nuts now."

The triangular drama quickly shifted into high gear. Jean and the Millers took a basement apartment together on Brooklyn's Henry Street, one door down from an alleyway called Love Lane. They festooned the walls with bizarre frescoes and painted the ceiling violet. In *Crazy Cock*, Miller says the air there was "blue with explanations": elaborate stories, contrived confessions, misleading tales were spilled forth over the apartment's "gut table." As we learn from *Crazy Cock*, June began to question Henry's sexual orientation, a habit that made her increasingly unstable husband furious. All three were by nature unbalanced—Jean had been institutionalized (as is Vanya in *Crazy Cock*), June was almost certainly a borderline psychotic, and Miller was beginning to wonder if his situation was a symptom of the same madness that had already institutionalized one member of his family. Both June and Jean used drugs, and the basement apartment took on the atmosphere, Miller wrote, of a coke joint. At night he often combed Jean's mane of black hair and pared her toenails; in the next moment he might embed a knife in her bedroom door. One night he was driven to a feeble attempt at suicide; June never even read the note he left for her.

This was the milieu Miller set out to capture in *Crazy Cock*. The novel ends with Hildred, Vanya, and Tony Bring still locked in their deadly triangle in the basement apartment. In Miller's life, this epoch ended one evening in April 1927 when he returned to find an empty apartment and a note saying the two women had sailed for Paris. During their absence, he composed the voluminous notes that would be transformed into a fictional account of his dehumanization at the hands of June and Jean. And, slowly, he began to recover. Two months later, June returned, without Jean.

A year—and a trip to Europe with June—intervened before Miller turned to the events of the winter of 1926–1927 and began writing *Crazy Cock*. June was now ready, she said, to make any kind of sacrifice necessary for him to succeed as a writer. She formulated a plan to send Henry to Paris, where he would, she hoped, write a novel that would make him famous and establish her as one of the muses of the ages. It was under these circumstances that he produced three versions of the novel, at first titled *Lovely Lesbians*. He would rework the manuscript several times over the next four years, deleting material and changing endings. He changed the title to *Crazy Cock*, so that it referred not to the two women but to Tony Bring. The vicissitudes of his own remarkable life, and not those of the other players in it, were his surest literary subjects, he had learned; it was an important discovery, for the "autobiographical romance" was to become Miller's preferred genre, his subject always his own life.

In February 1930, Miller arrived in Paris, leaving a copy of *Lovely Lesbians* with June, so she could take it around to New York publishers. June reported from time to time that various publishers were interested in it, but these announcements were as unreliable as any of her concoctions. Soon after his arrival, Miller had begun working on what he called his

"Paris book," the capacious, rollicking account of the down-at-the-heel narrator's adventures in Paris that would become *Tropic of Cancer*. Even when the "Paris book" was accepted for publication by Jack Kahane of the Obelisk Press, Miller was still trying to place *Crazy Cock*, sending it to Samuel Putnam at Covici-Friede.

By the time *Cancer* appeared in 1934, however, Miller had given up on his third novel. The manuscripts of *Crazy Cock* were all now in June's possession; he asked her to bring them on her final visit to Paris in 1932, but she forgot. At that point Miller was transmuting the elements of the story of his life with June in his epic *Tropic of Capricorn*; he would not return to the story of the ménage on Henry Street until he undertook the writing of *The Rosy Crucifixion* in 1942. He returned to America in 1940, eventually settling in California's remote Big Sur, where he lived in poverty as this country's most famous banned writer.

By then *Crazy Cock* seemed to have disappeared, dependent as its existence was on June's strikingly peripatetic habits. Sometime after her return from Paris, June married Stratford Corbett, an insurance man with New York Life. (By a strange coincidence, they honeymooned in Carmel, oblivious to Henry's presence in nearby Big Sur.) A bomber pilot in the Second World War, Corbett remained in the military after the war, and June followed him to military bases, first in Florida and then in Texas. There the marriage ended, and June made her way back to New York. She wrote to Henry in 1947 for the first time in fifteen years, and her news was not good. Her health was very poor; she suffered from severe colitis, and it was clear that her mental condition had deteriorated. She wrote regularly throughout the 1950s, thanking Henry for the small amounts of cash he was able to send her, and her letters—lodged in the Miller archives at UCLA—make for unsettling reading. She worked for several years for the city's welfare department without pay, hoping to get on the city employment rolls. She was nearly destitute and plagued by health problems; several times she reported that she suffered from severe malnutrition. Yet she took a warm interest in Henry's children and became very friendly with Lepska and then Eve, Henry's wives during this time.

In 1956, word reached Miller that June had been confined to Pilgrim State Hospital by one of her brothers after an incident that involved a television falling out of her window in an Upper West Side rooming house. Miller arranged for a New York couple, James and Annette Baxter, to visit June regularly after her release and attend to her material needs. Miller himself stopped to see June on the way back from a trip to Europe a few years later and found her horribly deteriorated, partially crippled by a fall suffered during a shock treatment at Pilgrim State. But he was struck by her courage; he believed that only sheer will had enabled her to survive.

Nobody thought to ask June about the manuscripts of Miller's early novels, those he had written during their marriage. Two trunks full of belongings had accompanied her throughout her travels, but she claimed the contents of one were ruined by water damage. Annette Baxter, however, was a Miller scholar—she had published her doctoral dissertation on his writing—and she convinced June that any manuscripts in her possession would have considerable interest. In December of 1960 the Baxters reported to Miller, with great excitement, that they had found the "Tony Bring" manuscripts. June, however, was reluctant to let them out of her sight. The Baxters investigated the feasibility of buying one of the recently introduced photocopying machines and had resolved to do so when June capitulated, turning over the manuscript *Moloch* as well. The Baxters sent them off to Miller with much fanfare.

But Miller's circumstances had changed considerably. Barney Rosset of Grove Press had mounted what was to be a successful challenge of the bans of Miller's books with the U.S. publication of *Tropic of Cancer* in 1961, and Miller had become an international celebrity. He was hoping to find a new home in Europe; when that did not work out, he settled in the Pacific Palisades neighborhood in Los Angeles. Rosset had a backlog of previously banned Miller titles to publish, and Henry decided not to show him his first writing efforts, which now seemed unimportant. Miller eventually sent them off to the Department of Special Collections at UCLA, where they remained, uncatalogued, for many years.

CRAZY COCK, for an apprentice work, is remarkably self-sufficient as a novel, requiring very little emendation. Miller has not mastered certain rudiments of narrative, so that, for instance, it is difficult to understand what is happening in the first twenty pages without knowing that they chronicle Vanya's journey east and her arrival on the Greenwich Village scene, and that they introduce Tony Bring, aspiring writer, and his wife, Hildred. Because so many drafts were produced, the narrative is not entirely consistent; verb tenses, for example, occasionally shift meaninglessly. But the narrative is far more linear than Miller's later work, even though it is marked by the often surrealistic verbal flights that characterize the *Tropic* novels and *Black Spring*.

One aspect of *Crazy Cock* does demand comment: the author's marked anti-Semitism. Words like "kike" and references to the "keen, quick, slippery Jewish mind" are not what we expect from a man who was deeply committed to equality and individual rights. In fact, Miller's early adulthood was characterized by a virulent, particularized anti-Semitism. He remembered his childhood in the Williamsburg section of Brooklyn as idyllic. With the opening of the Williamsburg Bridge, the character of the neighborhood changed, as waves of Italian and Jewish immigrants settled in Brooklyn. Miller came to hate the Eastern European Jew in particular, and what in a milder man might have festered as a grudging prejudice became in Miller a virtual obsession. Like many such obsessions, it was born out of a deep ambivalence, for Miller was drawn profoundly to many things Jewish, even at times wondering if perhaps he was Jewish himself. After World War II, Miller spoke of Jews sometimes with near-reverence and always with admiration. But in his earliest books—the *Tropic* novels and the two that preceded them—the author's anti-Semitism provides a shock far less pleasurable or meaningful than those we have come to expect from Miller.

With its descriptions of Village "faggots," its graphic portrayals of rape and clinical discussions of "perversity," its drawn-out description of Tony Bring's hemorrhoids, and its troubling references to Jews, *Crazy Cock* is an unsettling and disturbing book; it is also, as a testament to Miller's suffering, a profoundly moving book. Like his best work, it navigates a fine line between acceptance and rebellion, rejoicing and disgust; it represents a considerable artistic achievement from one of the most complicated men of the twentieth century.

—MARY V. DEARBORN
April 1991

Publisher's Note

THE PUBLISHING of posthumous fiction naturally presents special problems, and the reader is entitled to know what, if any, editing has taken place. We have earnestly sought to present this novel in as untrammeled a form as possible, correcting only misspellings, obvious inconsistencies, and verb disagreements where no rewriting was entailed. With these minor exceptions, this first publication of Henry Miller's third novel is exactly as he wrote it.

Author's Foreword

Apologies to Michael Fraenkel.

Preface

———◆———

Good-bye to the novel, sanity, and good health. Hello angels!

Part 1

1

———◆———

A REMOTE and desolate corner of America. Vast mud flats on which no flower, no living thing grows. Fissures radiating in all directions, losing themselves in the immensity of space.

Standing on the platform in her heavy cowhide boots, a thick, brass-studded belt about her waist, she puffs nervously at a cigarette. Her long black hair falls like a weight to her shoulders. The whistle blows, the wheels commence their smooth, fateful revolutions. The ground slips away on an endlessly slipping belt.

Below her a gray waste choked with dust and sagebrush. Vast, vast, a limitless expanse without a human being in sight. An Eldorado with less than one inhabitant to the square mile. From the snowcapped mountains that shoulder the sky strong winds blow down. With twilight the thermometer drops like an anchor. Here and there buttes and mesas dotted with creosote bushes. Tranquil the earth beneath the moaning wind.

"Taken as I am and as I shall always be, I feel that I am a force both of creation and of dissolution, that I am a real value, and have a right, a place, a mission among men."

She shifted languidly in her seat. The sensation of movement rather than movement itself. Her body, relaxed and quiescent, slumped deeper into the cushioned recesses of the seat. *Taken as I am* . . . The words seemed to raise themselves from the sea of type and swim before her muted vision in a colorless mist. Was there something beyond the screen of language which imparts to us . . . ? It was impossible for her to formulate, even to herself, the meaning of that flood which illumined for her, at that moment, the hidden places of her being.

After a time the words erased themselves from the inner pool of her eye; they vanished like the ectoplasm which is said to issue from the bodies of those who are possessed.

"Who am I?" she murmured to herself. "*What* am I?"

And suddenly she remembered that she was putting behind her a world. The book slid from her hands. She was again in the cemetery behind the ranch house, her arms clasping the trees; riding naked on a white stallion toward the icy lake; valleys everywhere choked with sunshine, the earth fecund, groaning with fruit and flowers.

IT WAS after the Krupanowa woman made her appearance that she chose for herself the name Vanya. Before that she had been Miriam, and to be a Miriam was to be a considerate, self-effacing soul.

The Krupanowa woman was a sculptress. That she possessed other accomplishments—accomplishments less easily categorized—was also conceded. The collision with a star of this magnitude flung Vanya out of her shallow orbit; whereas before she had existed in a nebulous state, the tail of a comet, as it were, now she became a sun whose inner chromosphere blazed with undying energy. A voluptuous ardor invaded her work. With bister and dried blood, with verdigris and jaundiced yellows, she pursued the rhythms and forms that consumed her vision. Orange nudes, colossal in stature, clawed at breasts dripping with slime and gore; odalisques bandaged like mummies and apostles whom not even the Christ had seen exposed their wounds, their gangrened limbs, their bloated lusts. There was Saint Sossima and Saint Savatyi, John the Warrior and John the Forerunner. Her madonnas she surrounded with lotus leaves, with golden groupers and leprechauns, with a vast, inchoate spawn. Inspired by Kali and Tlaloo, she invented goddesses from whose grinning skulls reptiles issued, their topaz eyes raised to heaven, their lips swollen with curses.

A singular life she led with the Krupanowa woman. Drugged by the ritual of the mass, they staggered to the slaughterhouse, thence to the lives of the Popes. They ran their fingers over the skins of cretins and elephants, they photographed jewels and artificial flowers, and coolies stripped to the waist; they explored the pathologic monsters of the insect world and the still more pathologic monsters of Rome. At night they dreamed of the idols buried in the morain of Campeche and bulls charging from the stockade to expire under straw hats.

HER PULSE quickened as the tumultuous procession of thoughts drove the bright warm blood full-crested through her veins. She looked at the book in her lap and saw again these words:

5

"Taken as I am and as I shall always be, I feel that I am a force both of creation and of dissolution, that I am a real value, and have a right, a place, a mission among men."

Suddenly, without let or warning, a dynamo broke loose inside her. Every particle of her molten being was convulsed with shuddering raptures. Mottled words drugged her with venomous lust. . . . She felt that in everything, sublime or ignoble, there was hidden a turbulent, a vital force, a significance and beauty of which art, however glorious, was but a pale reflection. "I want to live!" she muttered wildly. "I want to live!"

2

TONY BRING sat alone in a furnished room overlooking the harbor. It was midnight. That meant he had been two hours or more reading the same chapter. It was all very abstruse, an orgy of learning wrapped in ermine. He felt himself sinking deeper and deeper and the bottom nowhere.

It was only a few days ago that his friend had put this morphology of history, as it was called, in his hands. And now, he reflected, the body of his friend was quietly decomposing under a hummock smothered with roses.

He felt oppressed. It was not only that the spirit of his friend lay embalmed in the pages of the book, it was not only that the significance of the text was beyond him, it was that he could no longer tolerate the loneliness which came over him as he sat waiting to catch the sound of her steps.

This infernal waiting had been going on now for several weeks, not every night, it is true, but intermittently, and with a frequency that rasped his nerves. Down below, where the harbor expanded in a broad, inky splash, there was peace. The shagreened surface of the water, uniting with the pall of night, threw a screen of liquid silence over the earth. As he lifted the curtain aside to stare into the darkness he was seized with an inexplicable feeling of terror. It seemed to come upon him, as though for the first time, that he was utterly alone in the world. "We are all of us alone," he mumbled to himself, but even as he said it he could not help but feel that he was more alone than anyone else in the world.

At least, he told himself (he had been telling himself this repeatedly), there was nothing definite to worry about. Wasn't there though? The more he endeavored to reassure himself, the more convinced he became that there lurked a sinister misfortune whose reality and imminence was expressing itself in these tenuous, shadowy forebodings. Little comfort was there in the thought that the ordeal might be of limited duration. The question was whether it did not constitute but a prelude to a final, uninterrupted isolation. The periods of suspense, which in the beginning had a plausible span of an hour or two, were now stretching out to truly incommensurable lapses of time. By what calculus could one measure the sheer cumulative agony between an hour's wait and five? What could the passage of time, as indicated by the slow-moving hands of a clock, yield in problems of this sort?

But there were explanations . . . ? Yes, of explanations there was no end. The air at times was blue with them. Yet nothing was explained. The very fact that there were explanations required explaining.

His mind dwelt for a while on the complexities of that life which is lived in big cities—the *autumnal* cities—wherein there reigned an ordered disorder, a crazy justice, a cold disunity that permitted one individual to sit peacefully before his fireplace while a stone's throw away another was foully murdered. A city, he said to himself, is like a universe, each block a whirling constellation, each home a blazing star, or a burned-out planet. The warm, gregarious life, the smoke and the prayers, the clamor and parade, the whole bloody show was pivoted on a fulcrum of fear. If a man could love his neighbor he might have respect for himself; if he could have faith he might attain peace—but how, *how*, in a universe of bricks, a madhouse of egotists, an atmosphere of turmoil, strife, terror, violence? For the man of the autumnal cities there was left only the vision of the great whore, mother of harlots and abominations of the earth. *These shall hate the whore, and shall make her desolate and naked, and shall eat her flesh, and burn her with fire.* That was the revelation for the spiritually dead . . . chapter the last . . . book of books.

So absorbed was he in his reverie that when suddenly he turned his head, saw her standing at the threshold, he almost collapsed.

BENEATH HER purple smock she was nude. He held her at arm's length and gazed at her long, intently.

"Why do you look at me like that?" she gasped, still breathless.

"I was thinking how different . . ."

"You're going to begin that again?"

"No," he said quietly, "I'm not going to harp on it, but . . . well, look here, Hildred, sometimes you do look frightful, simply *frightful*. You can look worse than a whore when you try." (He lacked the courage to say plump out: "Where were you?" or "What have you been doing all this time?")

She went to the bathroom to reappear almost immediately with a small bottle of olive oil and a Turkish towel. Spilling a few drops of the oil into the palm of her hand, she proceeded forthwith to smear her face with it. The soft, spongy nap of the towel absorbed the dirt and grease which had collected in her pores. It looked like a rag on which an artist wipes his brushes. "Weren't you worried about me?" she asked.

"Of course I was."

"*Of course!* What a way to put it! And no sooner do I arrive than you tell me I look like a whore . . . worse than a whore."

"You know I didn't call you a whore," he said.

"It amounts to the same thing. You like to call me names. You're not happy unless you're criticizing me."

"Oh, don't let's go into that," he said wearily. He felt like screaming, "The hell with all this! Do you love me, that's all I want to know! *Do you love me?*" But before he could whip it out she was already lulling him with her deep, vibrant voice. Her tongue was fluent . . . too fluent. The throb of her dark, lush cadences pulsing through him like the warm blood of her veins awakened sensations that mingled confusedly with the meaning of her words. Darkly clustering, profuse and obscure, his thoughts penetrated hers and hung there behind the words, a veil which the slightest wind might rend.

3

———◆———

THERE HE sat, the villainous little duffer, with his golden locks and his pointy Chinese nails. He was almost in the show window, his back turned to the street. Remarkable what a ringer he was for John the Baptist. When he stood up and presented himself full on he changed suddenly into a mastiff, that intelligent sort that learns to walk on its hind legs after snatching a few pieces of raw meat. He wore a habitually placid expression. Either he had just fed well or he was about to feed well. An Oriental passivity. A glass lake, which if it rippled, would crack.

Vanya's broad shoulders and towering build almost hid him from view. It was comical to behold his solicitude. Seizing her hand, he wet it with his lips like some whelp licking the hand of its mistress.

An odor of rancid food was all-pervasive.

"Eat, Vanya, eat!" he implored obsequiously. "Eat all you want. Eat until you burst!" Hildred he politely ignored, or if he was obliged to address her, he elaborated his remarks with such flowery insincerity that she felt like strangling him. He had a way of drawing back his upper lip and smiling through his yellow teeth—a most revolting blandishment. "You look very charming tonight," he would say, "*very* charming," and turn his back before he had even finished the compliment.

A mild commotion was taking place because of the presence of a poet who insisted on shoving spaghetti into his vest pockets. In the last stages of intoxication, he was endeavoring to amuse a couple of females who were hanging on to him like vultures. Beneath their fur coats, which he opened occasionally, they were nude. The corners of his bloodshot eyes were filled with a whitish substance; the lids, which had shed their lashes, looked like sore gums. When he grinned there showed between his thick, shapeless lips a few charred stumps and the tip of a moist tongue. He laughed incessantly, a laugh that was like the gurgle of a sewer.

The sluts for whose ears his stuttering delicacies were intended regarded him with fatuous incomprehension. With regard to the other sex he acknowledged only one concern—that his women possess the organs essential for his gratification. Beyond that it mattered little whether they were brown or white, cross-eyed or deaf, diseased or imbecilic. As for that little duffer Willie Hyslop and his gang, one could not tell unless one looked below the waist, and even then the problem was complicated.

"Vile, disgusting creature!" Hildred exploded after they had left the cafeteria. "I don't see how you can tolerate him."

"Oh, he really isn't such a bad sort," said Vanya. "I don't see why you should despise him any more than the others."

"I can't help it," said Hildred. "It annoys me that you should permit him to use you."

"But I've told you, I'm broke . . . dead broke. If it weren't for him, the little fool that he is, I don't know where I would be now."

These remarks were passed on the street, at Vanya's door. Why does she stand here? thought Hildred. Why doesn't she invite me up?

As if divining her thoughts, Vanya shifted uneasily, grew

12

strangely embarrassed, and made vacillatory attempts to pro-
long the conversation. There was something on her mind
which she had been trying all evening to give expression to.
More than once she had attempted to approach the subject
obliquely, but Hildred was either obtuse or else unwilling to
render the smallest assistance.

"You would like to go to Paris with me, then?" said Vanya
impulsively.

"I would like it better than anything in the world. But . . ."

"Listen, you don't think it strange that I should talk to you
the way I did tonight?"

"I feel as though I had known you all my life." And then
suddenly she added quietly: "This is where you live?"

"For the present," answered Vanya, nodding her head.
They were silent a moment.

"Vanya," said Hildred, impulsively again and in a low,
eager voice, "Vanya, I want you to let me help you. You
must! You can't go on this way."

Vanya grasped Hildred's hand. They stood looking into
each other's eyes. For a full minute they stood thus, neither
daring to trespass beyond the spoken word.

Finally said Vanya calmly: "Yes, I will let you help me . . .
gladly . . . but how?"

Hildred hesitated. "*That,*" she answered, "I don't know
myself." The words dropped slowly, like flakes of snow from
her lips. "Just consider me your friend," she added earnestly.

Whether it was the effect of these last few words or a
determination to carry out a preconceived idea, at any rate,
Vanya turned abruptly and bounded up the stoop. Looking
down upon her somewhat startled companion, her friend,
she pleaded with her to wait. "Just a few minutes," she
begged. "I have something I want to give you."

4

In the beginning there were cow paths and the cow paths were all there was of the Village. Today she sprawls out like a sick bitch debilitated by an attack of delirium tremens. Dreary. Greasy. Depressing. Tourists dragging themselves along by the roots of the hair. Poets who haven't written anything since 1917. Jewish pirates whose cutlasses intimidate nobody. Insomnia. Cock-eyed dreams of love. Rape in a telephone booth. Perverts from the vice squad hugging the lampposts. Cossacks with fallen arches. A bohemian world jacked up with a truss. Hammocks on the third floor.

Every night, regular as clockwork, a rubberneck drew up in front of the Caravan and deposited its load. A fine goofy joint with atmosphere or what was left of atmosphere. Wasn't it here that O. Henry tossed off his masterpieces? And didn't Valentino come here, and Bobby Walthour? Who that had ever been anybody had not been here at one time or another? Why, Mary Garden herself had been known to swish majestically through this *Liebestod* of candle grease and burnt umbers. And Frank Harris—he with the luxurious mustachios and the pontifical swagger—was it not in this same bat-gloom that he sat listening to the tiresome pribble of his admirers? It was here that O'Neill nursed his lecherous dreams, here that Dreiser plopped, dour, morose, scouring mankind with his fierce, brooding eyes, eyes of melancholy, eyes of genius, any kind of eyes you want.

IT WAS well after the lunch hour when Tony Bring entered the Caravan. A tall girl with red hair was moving from table to table blowing out the candles. A piano tinkled in the corner. An underground life, he thought, as he scrutinized the sodden faces on which the shadows bit cruel marks of sloth and vice. Somehow, not the evil of existence but its dismal, thwarting aspect oppressed him. Veils of cigarette smoke collected in blue wisps and floated like thin chords of music above a screen of silhouettes. Here and there a candle sputtered its last, filling the room with an acrid, choking odor.

In the far gloom, drumming nervously with his thick fingers, sat a massive, stonelike figure. From a distance his features were not unpleasant; up close they had a frizzled, pounded look, as if they had come but an hour ago from the butcher's block. It was the face of a gladiator, worn down, crumbled, like a statue exposed to centuries of rain and frost.

Crush 'em quick—that was Earl Biggers' style. And the bigger they were the better he liked it. They could grease themselves all they liked. Once he caught hold it was curtains and a free ride to the hospital. But to see the glum look on his face at this moment one might well imagine that it was he who had been defeated last night. He was sore as a pup. Mechanically he felt of his ears, one of which was closed like a bud. A sour smile passed over his face. Another year of this, he said to himself, and I'll be fit for the zoo.

The girl with the red hair brushed by him. He grabbed her arm. "No funny business now," he said. "Tell me, where did that bare-legged bitch disappear to?"

"Don't be so rough," said the girl. "I told you she'll be back any minute."

"She's gone for a walk, I suppose . . . *with her friend.*"

"Yeah, *with her friend.*"

"Listen, if she wants something masculine, why don't she take me? Look at me! I'm a man, do you see?" And he blew out his chest.

Tony Bring, occupied with his own thoughts, paid no attention to the conversation going on, but there were others who were listening amusedly. His thoughts dribbled away into the gloom, taking neither form nor content.

As he sat there musing, Hildred fluttered in. Glued to her side was a tall, silent creature whose raven hair, parted in the middle, fell in a copious sweep to her shoulders. She was like a piece of marble not completely detached from the block.

"Hey, there!" came a big, booming voice. Hildred wheeled around instantly. The soft, waning light of the street suffused her face with a dull glow; about her lips there played an eager trembling, delicate, sensitive, a movement scarcely perceptible. As she moved toward him, buoyant and seraphic, he remarked the glow which radiated from her and transfigured her. So compelling was the vision that when a ponderous, apelike figure rose up between them and intercepted her it seemed as if a meaningless cloud had for a moment obscured his sight. He waited a moment, in that state of suspense which precedes disillusionment, and then, inexplicable and unbelievable though it appeared, Hildred sat down, sat down beside the ape and commenced talking to it.

A gesture of politeness, he assured himself, observing her quietly as she leaned forward, her face uplifted, her eyes flashing, when she laughed revealing her milk-white teeth, so smooth, so even. The hand which she had extended in greeting remained in the big, hairy paw which had closed over it. It was clamped there, as in a vise. And then he noticed that she was making an effort to free herself, but the other still held her hand. Suddenly, with her free hand, she struck out. The man's hand opened instinctively. The blood leaped to his face.

Now, he thought, she will surely get up and come over. At the same time he asked himself how often a scene like this took place. Was it really a reproof, that slap in the face? He waited. Waited for some sign of recognition. But her glance never once rested upon him. Not by the subtlest sign did she communicate to him an awareness of his presence. "Good God!" he muttered. "Could she have failed to see me?" Impossible! Why, she had looked straight at him, she had started toward him, and then this big ape had moved in and intercepted her. And the way she had looked at him! Such a look! Suddenly a black, damnable suspicion entered his mind. No, it was too preposterous—he dismissed it at once. She had seen him, all right, he was certain of it. Back of this malingering there was some deep reason, some purpose whose meaning would be made clear later on. Only too well did he understand the deceptions she was obliged to practice. What roles they had played, the two of them! Sometimes, when these fantastic situations passed through his head, he found it difficult to draw the line between pretense and actuality. So far, and this appeared as a comforting reflection, they had always played together, opposite each

17

other, as it were. He studied her now, as one would study an actress from the wings, while she sat talking to this idiot, enveloping him most likely in her clever net of deceit and falsehood. What was she saying to him? What sort of lies was she handing out? How candid and ingenuous was her smile—and yet it was no deeper than her lips. She was an actress, that wife of his, if ever there was one. A veritable honeycomb of dissimulation. . . . The more he watched her the more pleased he became. His pleasure was that of a child taking apart a complicated toy.

She was more beautiful than ever now. Like a mask long withheld. Mask or mask of a mask? Fragments that raced through his mind while he arranged harmoniously the inharmony of her being. Suddenly he saw that she was looking at him, peering at him from behind the mask. A rapport such as the living establish with the dying. She rose, and like a queen advancing to her throne, she approached him. His limbs were quaking, he was engulfed by a wave of gratitude and abasement. He wanted to fling himself on his knees and thank her blabberingly for deigning to notice him.

Her breath, warm and fragrant, filled him with terror and joy. Her low eager voice, throbbing and vibrant, smote him like a wilderness of stifled chords. While she excused herself hysterically he lowered his eyes as if to erase the confusion that had gathered there.

"You saw me, then, when you came in?" he asked, still somewhat abashed. His manner was like that of a lover keeping a clandestine engagement.

"Saw you?" she said. "What do you mean?"

"You didn't see me . . . ?"

"Didn't see you?"

18

Her perplexity was perplexing. Mask of a mask. Sphinx and Chimera joined in a protean act. The riddle remained a riddle, the riddle became a gladiator massacring the table, a stone-faced automaton with the lungs of a gorilla and bellows in his entrails. "Hildred!" he yelled. "Hildred!" Voice like a lion's yawn, deep, red mouth choked with rhododendrons.

"I'll fix him," said Hildred, rising quickly with white-surging anger. Her fingers twitched, as if they were already tearing the red mouth back to the ears.

He was still pounding the table when she approached.

"What is it, *stupe?*" she bawled out.

He recoiled—the gesture of a man trying to push a megaphone from his ear.

"What is it you want? Say something!"

"I want some attention, that's what!" he wheezed. "What's the matter, don't I give you a big enough tip?" Silence. "Listen," he chirped, and a roguish twinkle crept into his eyes, "who is that guy back there? Do you want me to bend him in half for you?"

"Idiot!" she cried, raising her voice. "Your brain is turning to muscle. Look at you . . . a wagonload of meat! Do you expect me to fall on your neck because you won on a foul last night? If you ever had a real tussle you'd fall apart. . . ."

There followed a few more gibes, galling, vicious, all of them directed below the belt. Big bruiser that he was, he wilted; there were tears in his eyes. He was silent as a clam; he put his head down, as though defending himself from a strangle thrust. Droll! The man of a thousand holds, giant with the body of a god, sinews of steel, flashing muscles, sitting there with his head drawn in like a turtle. Tame as a piece of putty. That's what it amounted to—a piece of putty in her hands. Everyone could see it.

Tony Bring looked on with embarrassment. And yet, as one of the clients was remarking in smothered whispers, it was comical to see how the man returned every day for his punishment. He seemed to thrive on it. Big, blustering, good-natured brute that he was, he would doubtless stagger in on the morrow, look the crowd over with that stony eye of his, and blurt out a hearty greeting in a voice to make the room tremble. He had a notion, moreover, that he could sing. Seeing Hildred, he would go to the piano and, resting his heavy paws on the keys, empty his bowels of a soupy love lyric. "Song of India" was his favorite air. Desperately he strove to lard the words with tenderness. But they fell out of his mouth like loosened teeth.

"Look at him!" said Hildred, after the excitement had blown over and she had returned to her place in the corner by the window. "Look at him! He's doubled up with grief and anguish. Good Lord, he's not blubbering, is he?"

"Please, Hildred, that's enough! Don't gloat over it."

"Don't tell me you're sorry for him," she said, her eyes flashing.

"I don't know. It makes me feel sick, like seeing a dog kicked in the stomach."

"Ridiculous!" said Hildred. "You haven't any idea what it's like dealing with these idiots."

"Perhaps. . . . But then I should think there were other ways. . . ."

A short, scornful laugh interrupted this. "You're a chump!" she said. "The idea, slobbering over a dope like that!

"The way you defend people," she added, "especially

people whom you have no right to defend, makes me ugly.'' Her voice had grown irritable and raspy. She turned abruptly and nodded her head. "See that woman over there with the white hair? If there's anything in the world I detest it's a prudish, sugar-coated bitch like her. She finds nothing but good everywhere. If you act nasty to her, if you insult her, she excuses you . . . tells you that you don't mean what you say. The old pfoof, she just pees over me with her sloppy gush. I hate people like that. I hate you when you defend people you don't know anything about. . . ."

Tony Bring made his usual efforts to control himself. She always talked this way when she got riled. The old woman was right—she didn't mean what she said. She was good, Hildred. She was an angel, but she was more comfortable when people regarded her as a demon. She was perverse, that's what it was.

"I don't think you should come here anymore." Hildred was talking again, more calmly now. "Really, Tony, I don't think you should. I don't."

He stiffened.

"Oh, I know it sounds strange," she continued, "but you mustn't try to invent reasons for what I say. Trust me, I know what I'm doing."

An anxious look stole into his eyes. Hildred was annoyed. He took everything so seriously. She softened immediately, however, and her voice grew even more suasive.

"This is all so stupid," she said. "I don't like to see you coming here, Tony. You don't belong here. Anyway, it won't be for long. You'll see. . . . I have a scheme up my sleeve. . . ." She looked at him sharply. "Aren't you listening?"

"I'm listening," he said. Schemes up her sleeves . . .

traps . . . snares. Everything bitched up from the beginning. Climax upon climax. Meaningless . . . meaningless. Fragments pieced together in irrelevant sequence. Bad dreams. "Yes, I'm listening. . . ."

He began to dream more violently, her words beating in unison with his thoughts. Half-thoughts they were, issuing in a larval stream that circulated over all the earth and through the waters beneath the earth. Because he was blind and had only a man's wisdom, because he humbled himself with truth and had no faith in her wiles, because in tomorrow he saw only the sordid chaff of yesterday . . . because of so many things foreign to his masculine comprehension the words that she tore from her breast came to him weighted with pain and bitterness.

Finally, in a voice from which all his manhood seemed to be drained, he said: "But aren't you the least bit glad that I came?"

"We're not discussing that," she said.

Like a blow her words struck him. As if he were standing at the head of a long flight of stairs and she had pushed him with all her might, left him stunned and helpless, the whir of bat wings ringing in his ears.

SOMEONE WAS standing beside them, at their elbows. It seemed to him as if the person had been standing there for an eternity.

"Oh, it's you!" Hildred exclaimed, looking up out of the corner of her eye. And immediately she grew flustered. "Tony," she said, "this is my friend. . . . This is . . . Vanya."

Later, when this incident had assumed its true proportions,

Tony Bring attempted again and again to reconstruct the details of this interview which was like a glimpse into a world hitherto unknown. But all that he could succeed in recapturing was the impression of a face—a face he would never forget—brought close to his, so close indeed that the features dissolved into a blur, the only thing standing out clearly in his memory being an image of himself squeezed into a space no bigger than a tear.

From now on it was Vanya this and Vanya that. Great swoops of volubility from Hildred, whose soul had departed the body to soar amid regions celestial and remote. From Vanya silence, deafening silence.

So this, he thought, is the Bruga woman, creator of that sunken-visaged, leering rake of a puppet which grinned at him night and day like a skulking lout. Well, he had a chance now to take a good look at her. . . . She was neither mad nor sane, neither old nor young. She had beauty, but it was rather the beauty of nature, not of a personality. She was like a calm sea at sunrise. She neither questioned nor answered. There were incongruities about her too. A da Vinci head stuck on the torso of a dragoon; steady, luminous eyes that burned behind torn veils. He gazed at her searchingly, as if to tear from her skull the cocoons constantly gathering in her eyes. A vital, hypnotic quietude. The stare of a medium, and the medium's voice. Her white neck was a little too long. It quivered when she spoke.

This meeting which, like an overture that threatened never to come to an end, left him hollowed out. His body was no longer an organism endowed with blood and muscle, with feelings and ideas, but a shell through which the wind whistled. Weird their language, like the flight of a whale at the sting of a harpoon when, quivering with rage and pain, it dives below the froth of the sea, its watery trail stained with blood.

He abandoned all effort to follow their words. His glance settled on Vanya's long goosey neck that vibrated like a lyre. So soft and smooth, her neck. Soft as vicuña. If you were left at the foot of the stairs, stunned and helpless, with bats whirring in your ears and a neck like that to fasten on, to clutch, to pray to . . . if you suddenly got up with rhodo-dendrons in your mouth, and your mouth torn back to the ears, if you had an organ in your entrails and the arms of a gorilla, arms that would crush blasphemously, ecstatically, if you had all darkness and night to roll in and curse and vomit and a neck beside you vibrating like a lyre, a neck so soft, so smooth, a neck sewn with eyes that pierced the veils of the future and spoke an unknown, an obscene language, if . . .

Part 2

Part 2

1

DAY BY day the shadows grew longer and the colors everywhere merged into golden browns and deep russets. Here and there objects stood out against the dull horizon with skeletal vigor: gaunt oaks twisting their licorice boughs in the gray pigment of sky, frail saplings drooping like scholars overloaded with wisdom.

As the days advanced a pall spread over the city; the wind roared through the deep gorges, whirling the dust and litter of the streets into choking spirals. The skyscrapers rose up with sepulchral gleam amid a haze of gray and rust. But in the cemeteries there was green, grass of resurrection, of life eternal. The rivers, too, were green, green as bile.

Each day brought new faces to the Caravan: brokers back from the Riviera, artists who had done a little sketching in the provinces, actresses with fat contracts, buyers from the fashionable department stores who had picked up a few phrases of French and Italian during their sojourn abroad. All preparing to burrow in for the winter, resume again the nervous, unhealthy life in which they pretended to find release and exhilaration.

Vanya practically lived at the Caravan. When Hildred

appeared in the forenoon Vanya was already there waiting to have breakfast with her. They met each day as if they had been separated for years.

Curiously enough, whenever Tony Bring dropped in they were gone. It was always the same story—Hildred has gone off somewhere *with her friend.* No mention was made of these visits until one day, just as Hildred was getting ready to leave the house, one of those tiffs occurred which were daily becoming more numerous. She accused him of spying on her. She knew only too well how often he had dropped in, the questions he launched, the sly insinuations. As a matter of fact, she had seen him herself now and then, pressing his nose against the windowpanes. God only knew where he didn't poke his nose.

Finally Vanya's name popped up. Vanya . . . yes, she was the one who had started all the trouble.

"You're jealous of her, that's what the matter!" cried Hildred.

"Jealous of *her*?" For a moment he was at a loss to find an epithet low enough to convey the full measure of his disgust. A fine friend she was, trying to worm her way in here and there with a pinch of dope, hanging out with whores and syphilitic poets. "Do you expect me to take her seriously?" he yelled. "A genius, you call her. What has she to show for her genius? I mean something more than dirty fingernails!"

Hildred heard him out in scorching silence. She was in the act of rouging her lips. Her face had a beautiful cadaverous glow; as she examined herself in the mirror she became intoxicated with her beauty—like an undertaker who perceives suddenly what a beautiful corpse he has under his hand.

Tony Bring was enraged. "Stop it!" he yelled. "Don't you see what you look like?"

She peered at herself calmly in the mirror. "I suppose I look like a whore, is that what you mean?" she answered sweetly.

Finally she was ready to go. At the door, her hand on the knob, she paused.

"I wish you wouldn't go yet," he said. "I want to say something. . . ."

"I thought you had finished."

He leaned against the door, squeezing her to him. He kissed her lips, her cheeks, her eyes, and the throbbing little pulse in her throat. There was a greasy taste in his mouth.

Hildred pulled herself away, and as she dashed down the stairs, she flung back: "Get a grip on yourself!"

MORE THAN once during the course of the night he jumped up, tossed aside the heavy volume he was reading, and dashed to the subway station. He waited in the arcade while one train after another pulled in. He walked over to the bridge plaza and waited some more. Cabs rolled by lugubriously. Cabs loaded with drunks. Cabs loaded with thugs. No Hildred. . . .

He went home and sat up the night. In the morning he learned that she had telephoned.

"What did she say?" he asked.

"She said she wanted to talk to you."

"Didn't she leave any message?"

"No, she just asked if you were home."

"That's all?"

"She said she wanted to talk to you."

As a reason for her absence Hildred explained that her mother had been taken ill.

O.K.

It was only several days later that he realized there were flaws in her story. When, acting on the impulse, he decided to telephone her mother he learned to his amazement that mother and daughter hadn't seen each other for over a year, that furthermore her mother didn't even know that her daughter was married.

When, several nights later while lying in each other's arms, he repeated word for word the conversation with her mother she commenced to laugh, she laughed as if her heart would burst.

"So my mother really said that?" Another gale of laughter. "And you swallowed it!" More laughter, slaughterhouse mirth. Then suddenly, abruptly, it was exhausted. He drew her to him. Her body was all atremble, dripping with perspiration. She tried to speak but there was only a gurgling in her throat. He lay very still and pressed her to him.

When she had grown very quiet he suddenly grasped her by the shoulders and shook her. "Why would your mother lie to me?" he demanded. "Why? Why?"

She commenced to laugh again, to laugh as if her heart would burst.

2

A FEW nights later he was called to the telephone. It was Hildred. Vanya had been taken ill and she thought she ought to stay with her. "Do you mind if I don't come home?" she asked.

"Yes, I do," he answered. "However, do as you think best."

A pause ensued during which he caught the remnants of a gabfest between two operators who had been on a bust the night before. When her voice floated over the wire again there was a strange quiver in it. "I'm coming home," she said. "I'm coming right away. . . ."

"Hildred!" he called. "Listen . . . listen!"

No answer. A buzzing in his ears mingled with the confusion in his brain. Just as he was about to hang up there came a faint, questioning *y-e-es?*

"Hildred, listen to me. . . . You go ahead and stay with her. . . . Don't worry about me."

"You're sure, dear? You're sure you won't feel badly?"

"Of course not! You know me . . . I'm just a big clown. Don't think about it anymore. It's all O.K. with me." As he hung up he added: "Have a good time!"

When he got back to the room he felt as if his guts were

dropping out. "I knew it!" he murmured. "I knew it was going to be something like that."

THE NIGHT seemed endless. Every few minutes he awoke and stared at the vacant pillow. Toward morning he fell into a fitful sleep. Dreams came in kaleidoscopic fashion; between pulse beats they came and went. Some he dreamed over and over, one particularly in which he saw her rolled up on a horsehair sofa, her face decomposing. How could a human being sleep so soundly when the face was decomposing? But then he perceived that her slumber was only a sort of thick pea soup, which made everything right again. . . . There was another dream in which he lived with an old Jew who shuffled about all day in his carpet slippers. He wore a patriarchal beard that floated in majestic waves over his sunken chest; beneath the beard there were jewels, a thick cluster of them, arranged like those in the breastplate of the high priest. When they caught the light the beard took fire and the flesh burned away to the skull. . . . Finally he dreamed that he was in Paris. The street on which he stood was deserted, except for a pair of streetwalkers and a gendarme who followed them like a pimp. At the foot of the street, where there was a sprinkle of lights, he could make out a carousel under a striped awning and a patch of green studded with marble fauns. Under the awning the lions and tigers stood rigid, their backs enameled in gold and ivory. Immobile they stood, while the music played and the fountain dripped its rainbow tints.

ON RISING he went straight to the Caravan. Hildred hadn't arrived yet—it was much too early for breakfast. He bought a paper and made for Washington Square. A few late ones were hurrying to work. He sat down on a bench. Foolish sitting there at that hour of the morning, cooling his heels in an empty square. He looked about listlessly. All the workers were at work. The drones were still in bed softly snoozing. Much too early for breakfast!

The air was crisp, invigorating. It was free, the air . . . one didn't have to pay a penny for it . . . not a mill. So Vanya was ill. The idea of that clodhopper taking sick struck him as ludicrous. God knows, women had their troubles, particularly when the moon and tides formed a mystic conjunction. Still. . . . In the *Encyclopaedia Britannica* it said that there was no such thing as a human hermaphrodite. A hermaphrodite was a creature containing both ovaries and testes. That was that. But Hildred knew a girl at the Caravan who had the stump of a tail. It was so, because someone had seen the young lady with her bloomers down. Some other young lady, most likely. . . .

When he returned to the Caravan there were three people seated at a table: a little boy, a woman of indeterminate age who appeared to be the boy's mother, and an elderly gentleman with a rapacious look who was engrossed in the task of picking his teeth. He observed that the little boy was unhappy. The idea of misery making its appearance at such an age was preposterous. He couldn't get it through his head at all.

The waitress came and took his order. Her face was fresh and rested-looking. Red apple cheeks and thick velvet strokes over the eyes. Marvelous to look at an eyebrow made of hair. He inquired if Hildred had arrived yet. No, none of the girls had shown up yet. "I'm the only one," she said smilingly. "I'm the early bird that catches the worms."

The worms? The expression struck him as remarkably thoughtless. He looked away and saw the little boy's mother smiling into the old man's eyes, smiling as if she had seen the Resurrection. Every now and then she turned to the youngster and pleaded with him to eat, but he merely rolled his eyes pathetically and wagged his little poodle dog's head. Tony Bring looked at the mother again. Strange, he said to himself, how women like to get themselves up like whores. At bottom they were all whores, every mother's daughter, even the angels.

The ten-o'clock breakfasters began to appear: nervous, little men, morose, preoccupied, who wiped their plates with crusts of bread; rude, massive women who, like primitive idols dug out of the soil, had grown rotten with the years; flowery dandies with repulsive faces, reminding him uncomfortably of illustrations in medical tracts. Everything he observed with sharp vigilance, with a cruel, remorseless eye. An old roué behind him was imploring the rosy-cheeked waitress to explain what a lamb's fry was. If only Hildred were here, he thought, she'd tell the horny old gaffer. *A lamb's fry!*

One by one the other waitresses dawdled in. They yawned and sneezed before they had so much as touched a plate. One of them sat down and tinkled the yellow keys. The notes dribbled from her fingers like sweat dripping from the wall. She sang in a weird, squeaky voice—"O there's Egypt in your dreamy eyes." The melody brought to her bucolic face the rapt expression of plugged nickels.

Eleven o'clock rolled around, and then a quarter after. No sign of Hildred, nor of Vanya. He inquired about her again. "Oh, Hildred—she's not coming in today," said the sickly looking bitch at the piano. "No, she's not coming in today, that's certain," she repeated. She smiled feebly as she spoke, like a gas jet filled with dust.

He stumbled out into the yellow light of the street cursing the Bruga woman for a hairy son-of-a-bitch, a gamboge go-devil with a rose-madder bladder. He prayed that all the evils of the Aztec calendar would fall on her coal-black mane. He prayed that her teeth would drop out one by one and the hair on her body grow longer. . . . As he walked away there drifted to his ears the tinkling of the yellow keys. Egypt's dreamy, seamy, squeamy eyes. He could still see the frail, brittle fingers from which the mildewed notes perspired and her soft spine bent beneath the weight of her addled brains, her teeth rattling like dice in a dice box.

A HALF hour later he was ringing Willie Hyslop's doorbell. No one answered. He hung around for a while, chatting with the children on the stoop. Then, in despair, he decided upon a thorough canvass of the Village. Cellars, garrets, speakeasies, studios, cafeterias—he hunted everywhere for them. Discouraged, he finally made his way back to the Caravan. It was like returning to the seat of a crime.

He learned that they had been in only a few moments ago. In and out again. He flew back to Willie Hyslop's dive over the bank on Hudson Street. Again he rang the bell. No answer. He walked across the street and stood gaping at the windows. Finally he sat down on a stoop opposite the house and fixed a blank gaze upon its weather-beaten facade. The street was choked with sewer gas. Concrete factories, shanties falling apart, dirty wash nocturnes. A desolate, crummy, woebegone bohemia. His limbs ached and over his thoughts there spread a thin, nauseous slime. Sewer gas. His brains stank. The whole world stank.

As he was about to make off an old woman approached him. She carried leaflets under her arm.

"Are you a Catholic, my good man?" she asked.

"I am not!" he answered.

"Excuse me, sir," she said, "but there's sadness in your face. May it do you good to know that Christ loves you."

"Christ be damned!" he said, and strode off.

In the subway he picked up a magazine that had been left on the seat. It was in German, and the cover was plastered with nudes. They all had big bottoms, like the women in Munich who spread themselves over the benches in the public gardens. He turned the pages at random. *"Guten Tag! Hat meine Kohlrübe heute nacht gut geschlafen?"*

The housekeeper met him at the door.

"Any message?" he asked.

The housekeeper was too parsimonious even to open her mouth. Besides, she had a watery blue nose. She was from Nova Scotia. As he bounded up the stairs, half suspecting that he would find Hildred lying in bed, the old witch commenced to scrape her throat. "Yes?" he shouted. "What is it?" He shouted not because she was hard of hearing, but to show his insolence.

She was informing him that the rent was overdue.

"Are you sure there's been no phone call?" he said.

"No," she replied. "Were you expecting one?"

3

━━━━━━◆━━━━━━

Vanya often got out of bed at night and walked the streets. She was frightened by shadows and heavy footsteps. She complained that at night the walls of her room collapsed like an accordion. She would not have flowers around for fear they would poison her. Colors affected her intensely. Faces also. There were periods when she was aware of nothing but noses. The odor of Lysol drove her to desperation. Soft-boiled eggs gave her the jaundice. . . .

Often she would lock herself in her room and, sitting before the mirror, apply the makeup of John Barrymore, Barrymore of *The Sea Beast* or of *Dr. Jekyll and Mr. Hyde.* Seeing these gruesome images in the mirror she would begin to rave. "Who am I?" she would say. "*What* am I?"

The notion that she might be a multiple personality intrigued her. Like an actress, she became weary of playing a single role, the role which fate had decreed her to play. She resembled those who imagine that by changing their address, or their name, they can alter the stupid course of their lives. Despite her age and her limitations, she had tried nearly everything. She had even tried to be a man.

It was difficult to keep track of her movements, her

repeated flights. Tony Bring, for example, had been laboring under the impression that he was camping on her doorstep a few nights previously. It is true that she had lived there once, but it is doubtful if Vanya herself would have recollected the place had it not been for an untoward circumstance which rooted it to her memory. This painful incident was a fire which had roused her from a dream wherein she imagined herself bathing in a bed of quicklime. Before she could convince herself that she was not dreaming, the fire had singed her chops. For several weeks thereafter she ate her meals standing up, and went to sleep on her belly.

In time a burn heals, but it is not so easy to get rid of the police. It seems that when the mattress caught fire a half-dozen occupants were driven from Vanya's room. Unfortunately three of them turned out to be androgynes; the other three were gynanders. Detectives were called in and the vice squad got busy with its slimy rubber gloves. Nobody would believe a word Vanya said. Finally Hildred lined up a politician and the affair was quashed. But Vanya's name was on the books. After a time she began to boast of the affair. She regretted that it was only "disorderly conduct" they had written beside her name.

Since this episode she had moved a number of times, and her name too she had changed several times. Little though Tony Bring suspected it, she was at present living only two blocks away from him in an old-fashioned brownstone house. The propinquity rendered it pleasant for Hildred to call for her on her way to work. Together they would breakfast at a nearby restaurant, disdaining the gratuitous meal at the Caravan, where they were obliged to eat under a more or less discreet surveillance.

Yet, intimate as these two were, Vanya did not fully share Hildred's confidence. She was unaware, for example, that her adored Hildred was married. When the fact was divulged to her she pretended not to believe it. Hildred was flattered. It was a delusion of hers that she was unattainable.

This farce, carried to absurd lengths, finally got under Tony Bring's skin. "If you don't tell her the truth," he said one day, "I'll tell her myself."

But Hildred succeeded in dissuading him. "You see," she remarked later, "I thought it would be safer to say that we were just living together. She knows I'm not a virgin. Besides, I can always have a lover, if I like. If I told her the truth, everybody in the Village would know that we're married."

And what was wrong with that, Tony Bring wanted to know.

"We can't afford to have it known—you know that as well as I," said Hildred testily.

That ended the matter—for the time being.

An hour or so later Tony Bring asked himself a question: *How did Vanya know that Hildred wasn't a virgin?*

4

ABOUT TWO o'clock one morning, shortly after this scene, the two of them walked in on him. He was in bed. Awakened by the creaking of the door, he opened his eyes and saw them standing in the doorway giggling. They had brought sandwiches and coffee.

While they ate, Hildred got a tub of hot water and made Vanya soak her feet. She wiped them tenderly and anointed them with cold cream. He looked on in astonishment. Vanya was taking it all as a matter of course.

"Look," said Hildred, "aren't they dreadful sores?"

Vanya raised her feet nonchalantly and yawned.

"It's nothing," he said, "just a slight irritation."

Hildred was indignant. With comb and brush she now devoted herself to untangling Vanya's mane. Vanya slumped down in the easy chair looking as contented as a bitch having her fleas removed. Tony Bring kept his eyes on Hildred, on the pale yellow prongs in her hand wandering lovingly through the blue-black moss. His thoughts followed vindictively. . . .

It had been decided—Hildred had decided it—that Vanya would stay overnight. The lights were extinguished. Vanya lay in one bed, he in the other. They had only to stretch their arms to join hands. Hildred moved about uneasily.

A struggle was going on. They were all struggling together—struggling with each other, struggling with themselves, struggling desperately not to struggle. Presently, like a wave that has traveled from under the rim of the horizon, Hildred flung herself between them. As she leaned over to kiss him goodnight, her body all flowers and moonlight, he felt a sickening desire to strangle her.

Now and again he opened his eyes and stared at the swooning figures huddled in the cloudy mass of bedclothes. Vanya's head floated in a pool of ink on Hildred's bosom. Her bare arm hung in a lazy coil over Hildred's billowy form. It was a strong, massive limb whose weight rested on the body of his wife like an anvil.

In the morning they invited him to have breakfast with them. He yielded as an invalid submits to the attentions of a nurse. The breakfast was an ordeal. He felt that he was in the way. The world was not big enough to contain the three of them. On the way to the subway they talked excitedly about a multitude of disconnected things. They pretended to be calm and unconcerned; they talked without saying anything, they listened to each other without understanding a word.

In the subway Hildred regained her self-possession. She stared about her with insolent defiance, raised her voice immoderately, and shouted things that one usually whispers, provided one has the temerity to mention them at all in public. With a devastating glance she would single out a face and analyze its background of vice or hypocrisy; elderly women especially, on whose features pity and horror were commingled, she challenged with ribald laughter and a malicious glare that made them wince. Vanya carried herself with the dignity of a ridiculous statue.

Emerging from the subway they ran straight into Willie Hyslop and his friends. Tony Bring tried to stand aside, but Vanya took him by the arm and introduced him ceremoniously. The situation reminded him of what a skeptic must endure when he is given extreme unction.

He listened attentively as the two called Toots and Ebba recounted their exploits. They had an alert, bristling air, like a pair of Airedales sniffing each other. They were attractive, too, in a bestial way. The nipples of their breasts pushed through their jerseys like fistulas.

At the door of the Caravan he drew Hildred aside and spoke to her in an undertone. She was out of sorts.

"But why did you do it?" he insisted. "That's all I'm asking. Can't you answer me that?"

Hildred was watching Vanya out of the corner of her eye. She explained very lamely that it would have been embarrassing to climb into bed with him in the presence of another woman. That got him. "You call that punk a woman?" he said hoarsely. Her face darkened. She began to brazen it out. Finally she took to calling him names. A look of pain came into his eyes. He felt sorry for her, and for himself, for everyone in the world who had to suffer when it was so unnecessary to suffer.

Suddenly, with a furtive gesture, she pressed his hand. "Can't we talk it over later?" she begged. So softly she said it, as if she were actually down on her knees before him.

He thought a moment. He wanted to be decent and fair about it. Maybe, as she had said, he *was* making a mountain

out of a molehill. The devil knew, he wasn't certain anymore
of what he was doing.

The others were watching now. She drew her hand away
quickly.

"All right," he said, "we'll talk about it later. But"—he
drew her further aside—"I'll say this now. . . . It doesn't
matter what you tell me, a thing like that can never happen
again . . . *never*, do you understand?" He turned and walked
away quickly.

She stood watching him as he walked off with quick,
resentful steps. A deep flush mounted to her cheeks. The
glare of the street made her eyes smart. She hated the sunlight . . . hated it . . . hated it.

As he walked away his mind was filled with bitterness and
disgust. He recalled how the one called Toots had walked up
to Hildred and kissed her on the lips. And only the night
before, according to her own words, she and Ebba had staged
an exhibition for some old billy goat, some rich, jaded idiot
who was curious about curious things. And there was Willie
Hyslop's yellow teeth and the silken mustache which had
just begun to sprout, which exaggerated his effeminacy. They
had dirty mouths, all of them, mouths which, erroneously or
not, the world associates with degenerates. He wondered
why he hadn't walked away from them at once. He rubbed
his perspiring hands on his overcoat as though to remove the
danger of contamination.

5

RETURNING HOME unexpectedly one afternoon he was astonished to find a pair of sleeping beauties in his bed. They lay like angels exhausted by heavy and incessant flights. He looked sharply at Vanya; she was struggling to keep her eyes shut. Hildred pretended to be snoring—she was snoring hard enough for a regiment.

Five minutes later he was rolling over the Brooklyn Bridge. White jockeys with spurs of malachite were scudding through the low-hanging clouds that hung like collars of fat about the slender ribs of the skyscrapers. The creaking wharves below plowed the leaping flood like blunt-edged combs. From the Battery to the bridge, like one vast fantasy in stone, the city wavered and trembled, shivered, shuddered, quivered with ecstasy. Between the black crevices, far, far below, moving like intoxicated ants, the city's millions swarmed.

At Sheridan Square he dismissed the cab. He became part of the throng whose activity at this hour of the day rose to the surface like a creamy, rose-tinted froth. At this very moment, in every part of the world, people were dreaming or talking about New York. New York! What was it made people so damned silly about New York? The swirl and jelly-dance on the sidewalks, the magnificent prisons blotting out the sky, the rancid smells, the razzle-dazzle . . . what? . . . just what? Here he was in the thick of it and not a drop of joy or pride in his heart. The beautiful women of New York . . . where were they? He saw only faces laid out with the monotony of graves, graves smothered with wreaths which had lost their perfume; they walked along like sawdust dolls galvanized by a swig of gin, wax virgins who had no virginity, bargain hunters pricked with the itch of possession, their cool, calculating faces registering a perpetual "To Let" expression.

Outside the bohemian joints stood ridiculous figures buried in ridiculous costumes. How should one suspect that the wretch one brushed against in the doorway would be only too glad to dispose of a corpse for a five-spot, that the first female one encountered harbored in her body the active germs of all the venereal woes, or that the suave gentleman with the cauliflower ear, who escorted you to a table, was a Borgia raised to the nth degree? Behind the velvet there might be enough gats to decimate an army corps.

Not far from Jefferson Market he came upon a modest three-story building; it was entirely dark except for a gleam no bigger than a knife blade coming from the ventilators in the basement windows. He stood before a heavy iron gate and rang the bell. The proprietor himself came to the door, peered through the grating, and after a nod of recognition turned on a pink light in the vestibule and unbarred the gate.

The place was jammed. It was always jammed. In the rear of the basement was the kitchen, in the front a bar about the size of a coffin. A genial buzz of voices greeted his ears; the faces were cheery and the beverages looked colorful and inviting. He stood a moment at the threshold, soaking up the warm, liquid glow of the room. They were standing three deep at the bar, the women outnumbering the men. Everyone seemed to be gay and tipsy. A woman was scratching her behind; she saw him look at her but it made no difference. It was her behind and she had a right to scratch it, since it needed to be scratched. A sort of proclamation of emancipation. . . .

As he was about to ascend the stairs leading to the dining room a tall, well-proportioned female, lit up like an ocean liner, started waddling down. She smiled heavily and gave a signal to stand clear. Her dress was high at the bottom and low at the top; she kept hitching it up as if she feared she would trip. Slowly and cautiously she lowered herself—like a grand piano. And all the while she smiled, as people smile when they're paralyzed. He stared straight into her eyes, and then a little lower, at the expanse of flesh between her knees and her waist. It was solid, olive meat polished here and there by glowing patches of shadow. He glanced from her thighs to her face and back again. She raised her skirt a little higher; her grin spread wider. She was ages hoisting herself down. She wasn't just lit up—she was fumigated.

"Have a drink?" she said, soon as she realized she had hit the bottom. He tried to refuse politely. "Oh, come on . . . have one!" she said, and he felt her thigh pressing against him.

"All right," he said, "but just one."

"Hell no, one won't do you any good. Let's have a flock of them. I'm sitting upstairs with a bunch of old hens. We're having a regular old hen party . . . ain't that fierce?"

"Yeah, fierce!" he said.

"Say, I don't look like an old hen, do I?" She squeezed his

arm in her painfully playful way. "Tell me," she repeated, "do I look like an old hen to you?"

"I wouldn't say you did . . . except for the feathers."

"Feathers? What feathers? Say, you're full of feathers yourself." With this she gave a lurch that nearly tipped him over.

They ordered martinis. She insisted on paying. The woman always pays. He looked at her dumbly and wondered where she was putting it all. The room was spinning; he had to watch her mouth to get what she was saying. The voices came to him in a confused blur splintered now and again by the staccato shouts of the waiters. They were lapping it up like flies at the bar. There was no need to hold himself erect; everyone leaned against everyone else. He was not so befuddled, however, but that he could tell whose hand it was pressing against his thigh. It was a hot, heavy hand, and every once in a while it got spasms or something. When he shifted a bit he felt her legs moving in and squeezing hard.

"Are you feeling all right?" he asked.

She grinned and her legs twitched some more. "Let's get out of here," she said, and taking him by the hand she led him toward the stairs. "Jesus, your hand's cold," she said. "Feel me . . . I'm hot as hell."

The idea of going upstairs to join a bunch of old hens didn't appeal to him at all. He tried to pull away from her. "Come on," she whispered. "I know what I'm doing." When they got to the second landing she stopped short. He saw a pink light over the door at the end of the hall. She had her hand over his mouth and was pressing heavily with her drunken weight. He raised his eyebrows questioningly toward the pink light over the door while she wagged her head from side to side like an automaton. Suddenly, chewing her lower lip, she gripped him tight. What the hell! he said to himself, feeling more and more like a pile of wet sand. The next moment he felt her lips fastened to his ear, her breath scorching. "Do it here," she murmured as she pressed him against the banister and with a convulsive, shuddering movement lifted her dress.

HE DIDN'T know where he was walking, only that it was somewhere uptown. He was famished and his head was still cloudy. But the frost soothed like an ice pack. There were a million lights—they dazzled and blinded him. They were little and then they grew big and swooped down on him. The colors were wild and dangerous. They rushed up on him like a flock of semaphores.

A sheet of ice, no thicker than the band of a ring, covered the asphalt. It was a mirror broken into an ocean of light waves, a mirror in which all the colors of the rainbow flashed and danced. A theater loomed up; the lobby had vertigo. It was not a lobby but a huge illuminated funnel revolving at high speed; into this dizzy, crystal maze long queues advanced with an undulating motion, like gigantic waves flinging their plumed crests against the shore of an inlet. With each smashing assault they eddied back in a swift-rushing vortex, were reabsorbed and became another column which in turn lifted its vibrant, hissing mass and broke in swirling cubes of light. . . . At a drugstore he saw a row of telephone booths in the window. The booths were put there to make people telephone. "I want to speak to Hildred," he said, when they had connected him with the Caravan. "She's not here," came a gruff voice. Bang! The receiver clicked like an automatic. He jiggled the hook. "Hello! Hello!" There came to his ears the hum of far-off planetary orbs rolling through ethereally cushioned space. It's no use, he said to himself, we're traveling in different orbits. The world was simply a field of blind energy in which microcosm and macrocosm moved according to the caprice of a demented monarch.

By the time he reached Times Square he was drunk with well-being. He felt the ebb and flow of bright, liquid blood in his veins. With trip-hammer rhythm it rose and fell, dilated his heart, bathed his vision, surged through his pulsing limbs. Bright, red, liquid blood: in a state of euphoria it made men wise, lucid, sane; diluted it produced flaccidity, neuroticism, despair, and melancholy; clotted it gave the spangled phenomena of solipsism, the terrors of epilepsy and chorea, the hierarchies of caste, the unfathomable magnitudes of dementia. In a single red corpuscle were sufficient enigmas to confound all the colleges of science. In blood were men born and in blood they died. Blood was potent, fecund, magical. Blood was an ecstasy of pain and beauty, a miracle of creative destruction, a particle of the divine essence, perhaps the essence itself. Where blood flowed life ran strong. Where there was song there was blood, and where there was worship there was blood. There was blood in the sunset, in the flowers of the field, in the eyes of maniacs and prophets, in the fire of precious gems. Everywhere where there was life and song and drunkenness and worship and triumph there was blood.

In this state of bloody exuberance he took a stand across the street from the Caravan. It was about midnight. Groups of idlers, attracted by the bursts of revelry escaping from the partially opened windows, clung to the railing in front of the establishment. Presently he was hanging on the railing himself. The privilege of enjoying this spectacle from the outside gave him a strange exhilaration.

Whenever Hildred brought to light an interesting personality she would escort him to a little niche in the corner near the window. Here, with elbows planted well forward, she would sit and stare admiringly into the eyes of the one who had for the moment captivated her. If, as had happened before, she averted her gaze for an instant and allowed her glance to stray through the window, lighting with a rapt, unseeing expression on the figures huddled at the railing, Tony Bring would lean forward involuntarily and wait with drunken heart to detect a gleam of recognition in her luminous eyes.

But tonight, this niche in which Hildred, like a patron saint, was accustomed to sit enshrined was vacant. He went inside and ordered food. There was a roach in the food but he was too hungry to wait for another order. Presently Earl Biggers came along, his massive form wedging through the tables like a piece of granite slipping down a mountainside. With him was a coarse-looking woman who posed as a French *vedette*. He recognized her immediately from the description Hildred had once given him. As Hildred said, there was a certain something about the mouth and eyes which, in spite of the woman's coarseness, made her attractive. It was common knowledge that she had a passion for robust, athletic males. She had also the foulest tongue of any woman on the American stage—a compliment of the first magnitude considering the competition to which she was subjected.

He watched intently as she trained her large, wicked eyes

on the assembly. One could hardly call them eyes, since they were not so much instruments for perceiving objects as huge, revolving drums of light which, skillfully directed, threw an argent flood over the frieze of faces. If one of the loose remarks which were constantly passing her lips awakened a response her nostrils dilated and quivered, precisely like a mare's in heat.

Someone showed her a book. "I read it," she said, and the enamel of her teeth gleamed lasciviously.

"Did you like it?" she was asked.

"Did I like it? Say, when I got through with that book I was playing with myself."

Earl Biggers was blushing. "You're a darling," she said. "You're so big and healthy you're going to spoil if you don't do something about it," and she squeezed his legs under the table.

At this moment a rather notorious female with a monocle in her eye walked in. Biggers pointed her out as the mistress of a prominent Broadway actress.

"Is that so?" she blurted out, loud enough for all to hear. "Say, I'd like to meet that dame. That's one thing I haven't tried yet."

The one to whom this remark had been obliquely directed, far from considering herself insulted, commenced thereupon to preen herself. Tony Bring looked at the cockroach he had laid to one side. He lost his appetite.

HILDRED WAS already undressed when he walked in. Her face was cold-creamed and there was a cigarette dangling from her lips.

"Where have you been?" she asked. She seemed upset.

Before he had time to answer, she added: "God, I don't know what to do. . . . Vanya's disappeared!"

"That's wonderful," he said. "I hope she's drowned herself. . . . And *you*," he added, "do you know what I think about you? I think you're crazy. I think if I had any sense I ought to strap you down and beat the piss out of you. I think I'm crazy, too, for tolerating all that I have. I swear to Christ if that woman appears again I'll mutilate her. And I'll fix you, too, mark my words. You've been driving me nuts with your goddamned Vanya this and Vanya that. Vanya be damned! She's disappeared, you say? Good. I hope she's croaked. I hope they don't even find a toenail. I hope she's stuck in a sewer and her body full of rats. I wouldn't care if all New York got poisoned so long as she's out of the way and done for. . . ."

6

YES, SHE had disappeared. As completely as if the earth had
opened up and swallowed her. Hardly had the news gone
around when it was announced that she was in Taos, but this
was immediately contradicted by a rumor that she had been
seen in an opium dive on Pell Street. Then, one day, a letter
arrived. "Dear Hildred," it ran. "I am in the psychopathic
ward here. One of the nurses has been kind enough to smug-
gle this out for me. Please come immediately—I'll go crazy if
they keep me here another day. The nurse says that I will be
released if someone appears to vouch for my conduct. Bring
some clothes with you—*something feminine.*"

This missive reached Hildred at the Caravan. Immediately
she took one of the girls aside and borrowed from her a suit
and hat. In the dressing room she removed the Vaseline from
her eyelids and the heavy strokes of soot from her eyebrows
and the alizarin from her lips and the green layer of powder
from her cheeks. Then she hurried out and bought a pair of
silk hose and bloomers.

Somewhat more conventionally garbed than usual, she
presented herself at the hospital. Dr. Titsworth, whom she
was instructed to see, was like most public officials engaged.

An elderly woman who appeared to be his secretary bustled to and fro with corpselike gravity. She had a high stomach over which she peered through magnifying glasses. Hildred gave her the once-over and turned her back on her.

The Under Secretary of the Insane appeared.

"You wished to see Dr. Titsworth?"

Hildred nodded.

"About what, please?"

"I'll tell that to him."

"But he's engaged just at present."

"Then I'll wait."

She was sitting on a hard, shiny bench. It was a tremendous barren hall with reformatory windows. She was getting hysterical looking at the bare walls; she was thinking what a place Vanya would make of it if they gave her a free hand. She hated the stained-glass windows: they reminded her of churches and toilets.

Presently the grand mogul was ushered in. He had the skull of a Caesar and the snout of a Czar. He extended his hand; it was like a piece of cold steak. They sat down and Hildred explained her presence, quite calmly and briefly. While she talked he drummed with his long, tapering fingers on the arm of the chair.

"What right have you to demand her release?" he asked.

Hildred replied that she was her legal guardian.

"Ah, I see! And you are how old, may I ask?" His tiny, gimlet eyes bored clean through her. It was an expression he had learned to assume in the presence of his patients. It was intended to make one uncomfortable.

Hildred toyed with the suede gloves she had borrowed and repeated the usual feminine gesture of covering her knees. Dr. Titsworth coughed modestly. He reminded Hildred very gently that it was entirely in his power to restrict the patient's freedom if he had a mind to, that is, if he was convinced that it was still necessary. Hildred listened very gravely and respectfully; she put her hand on his, quite accidentally, and then apologized profusely. Oh, it was clear that she was quite beside herself, that she had never found herself in such a predicament before.

"Doctor," she said, and her eyes were like angels weeping, "this affair puzzles me completely. I don't make a thing of it. I feel absolutely helpless, wretched. And doctor, didn't you say a while ago that you wished to ask me some questions?"

Titsworth immediately summoned his secretary and had a typewritten list, prepared in advance, brought to him. He held the paper absentmindedly in his lap, just long enough for Hildred to scan it quickly. They were the usual idiotic questions which, more than answers, require rubber stamps, seals, and the illegible scrawls of illegitimate witnesses.

Suddenly his beady eyes shifted slyly. "Now tell me, please," he said coldly, "how long has she been taking drugs?"

"Why doctor!" Hildred looked not only astonished, but injured.

"Come, come!" he said. "Why did she rave about Nietzsche when she was brought here? Why does she insist that Nietzsche drove her mad?"

"But doctor . . ."

"I suppose you know," Titsworth went on rapidly, "that your ward was raped the other night?"

Hildred gasped.

"That was a thing you didn't know, eh?" said Titsworth. "Why did you leave her that night? Why didn't you notify the police? Why . . . ?" There seemed to be no end to his questions. Then, as though he had had his amusement, he ceased abruptly and beckoning to a nurse issued a brief command. It seemed to Hildred as if it were the next moment that Vanya stood there, in the doorway, hesitant at first, then wildly exuberant. Her hair had grown longer; there was almost a bloodthirsty look about her.

"Hildred!" she cried. "You *did* come!" She almost pushed the latter over as she fell into her arms.

"Steady, Vanya, steady!" Hildred whispered as they clung to each other.

"God, Hildred, I thought you'd never come. I've been watching the clock all day. . . . You must come back to the ward—they're all dying to meet you. Wait till you meet George Washington . . . she's a scream!"

"Careful, Vanya!" said Hildred, giving her a swift nudge. Then, raising her voice, "You're very nervous, dear. It must have been terrible for you."

Vanya squeezed her hand.

"Don't worry, Vanya," said Hildred, "everything is settled. You're coming home with me."

Titsworth took it all in without opening his mouth. As they were going back to the ward a group of nurses passed through the hall. "Hello there! Hello everybody! I'm leaving . . . I'm leaving!" shouted Vanya. Then, clutching Hildred's arm, she whispered: "See that little blonde—she's got a crush on me. That's how I got the note out."

TONY BRING received the news soon enough. Hildred voiced her intention immediately of bringing her ward to live with them. There was a scene. For an hour or more they fumed and ranted. Finally he brought his fist down. "No!" he said. "Absolutely no!"

Then Vanya dropped in on them. She spoke to him softly and wistfully. Her eyes were still a trifle mad—large, restless orbs floating in green ink. Her speech still retained traces of that queer accent which Titsworth had mentioned to Hildred. She was changed. There was a subdued, frightened air about her.

There were days when Hildred did nothing, except to take her ward to the theater, or to a concert. There was the inevitable taxi bill and trifles like gardenias and orchids. If Vanya so much as sighed, Hildred was disturbed. Her slightest whim was immediately gratified. Thus when Vanya expressed a longing to paint again Hildred flew off and purchased a bewildering array of materials. Everything of the best. An ordinary easel wouldn't do—not for a sick genius. It had to be something out of the common run of easels. What she brought home was an elaborate affair of Javanese workmanship which, so she said, she had picked up for a song. Everything expensive was picked up for a song.

Looking at the situation with eyes wide open, Tony Bring asked himself one day what difference it could possibly make if they did establish a *ménage à trois*. True, he had refused to permit Vanya's trunk to be moved in, but what of that? Did that prevent her from sleeping with them, from using the same bathtub, from wearing his ties occasionally or criticizing the economy of the household?

7

---◆---

"*THEY WERE* crazy, not me! They strapped me down for I don't know how long. I couldn't breathe. I begged them to let me up—for five minutes—but they only laughed at me. In the next bed was George Washington. 'Let me call you sweetheart, I'm in love with you. . . .' Night and day she sang it. She drove me crazy, that woman. All day, all night—*sweetheart . . . sweetheart*. I couldn't stand it any longer. I exploded.

"Jesus, do you know what it's like to be strapped down? No, you don't! You can't imagine it. You kick, you holler, you curse. They come and shake their heads at you . . . they laugh. They make you believe you're crazy, even if you're not. After a while you get worn out . . . you quiet down. And then you pray. You don't know what you're saying, but you beg, you whine, you crawl like a worm. And then they come again with their cold, lizard eyes and they look down at you foolishly and they yell, 'Be quiet! Shut up!' You curse and swear, you beg, you whimper, you promise everything, but all they say is 'Be quiet! Shut up!'

"See! See these marks! That's what those dirty blood-suckers did to me. Wait . . . I'll show you more. Hildred, you saw my breasts . . . what did they do to me? I'll kill them someday, the dirty brutes!

"They'll remember me, all right! Twice I broke loose on them. The second time I cut George Washington loose. The whole ward went crazy. We broke the windows, we danced, we sang. . . . We put the fear of Christ in them, I tell you. . . ."

Vanya's fevered brain was twitching like a frog under the scalpel. Though she had narrated the story for the fourth or fifth time she insisted on going over it again . . . she wanted them to know everything . . . she was afraid always of overlooking some detail.

What happened the night that Hildred deserted her friend Vanya? Why did Hildred permit her to go off with a stranger, especially when Vanya was drunk and unable to take care of herself? Was she jealous of her good friend, or did she have an appointment with someone else? And why was she so sure that Vanya had disappeared? These were some of the questions that Tony Bring could find no solution to. It was he who encouraged Vanya to relate her experiences. He egged her on slyly, adroitly, despite Hildred's protestations. He pretended to be moved, he applauded her when she was dramatic, he soothed her when she was at the breaking point. He would excuse himself and go to the bathroom in order to make notes. He would return and wind her up again, remind her of things she had forgotten, trip her up when she contradicted herself, agree with her when he knew that she was lying. . . .

As the story pieced itself out, this, briefly, is what took place. Vanya, Hildred, and the man, who was an utter stranger, had had a few drinks together at the Caravan. Hildred left abruptly after a silly exchange of words with

Vanya. The man offered to escort Vanya to her door. When they got in the cab he ordered the driver to go uptown. Vanya pleaded with him to drive her home but instead of paying attention to her he proceeded to hoist her on his lap. A rumpus ensued. Before she knew what had happened she found herself on the floor of the cab, the man on top of her, beating her and twisting her arms. When she came to she was lying on the sidewalk beside a pump. She sat there for a while, dazed, searching her pockets for her keys. Finally she picked herself up and limped away. A clot of blood was stuck to her temple; she picked at it absentmindedly as she walked along.

She couldn't get her bearings—the streets were deserted and the names of the streets were unfamiliar to her. After a while there loomed up out of the grime and mist a scramble of hulls and sheds and funnels and masts. A helpless, frightened feeling invaded her. Perhaps she wasn't in New York anymore. Perhaps she had been shanghaied. Presently she heard a truck rolling up behind her. She beckoned to the driver. The truck stopped and she climbed up on the front seat. It was a moving van and there were two men—Polacks, she thought—sitting with the driver. She asked them to drive her to the Brooklyn Bridge and they agreed. After that not a word passed between them. They didn't ask her what had happened to her or what she was doing or anything. Not a peep out of them. She was terrified. She wondered if they were really taking her to the Brooklyn Bridge—and if they weren't? She didn't wonder how she would get away. She simply didn't think. She just kept mum and shivered. There wasn't anything in her head except a vague, paralyzing fear. Her brain felt as if it were petrifying.

Finally the van stopped. Immediately four or five huskies

spilled out of the interior of the vehicle. One of them reached up and pulled her off the seat. He carried her indoors. It was pitch-dark inside. A match was struck and then someone poked around in the corner where there was a bottle with a candle stuck in it. The men began to speak—quickly, and with low ejaculations. She couldn't understand a word. They seemed to be speaking several tongues.

During this brief interval she hadn't opened her mouth— she hadn't even made a gesture of protest. Suddenly she said to herself, I must scream, and she tried to scream but there came from her throat only a faint scraping sound. Immediately she felt a big, hairy hand, full of sweat and dirt, clap itself over her mouth. Almost at the same moment her clothes were whisked off. For a moment they left her standing there in her stocking feet while they put their heads together and held a brief, unintelligible consultation. Her stockings were slipping down; she bent over and pulled them up. Perhaps a minute went by while she stood there naked, her stockings neatly pulled up. Suddenly an arm was slipped under her knees and she was given a toss. She felt her spine crack as it hit the tabletop and there was a hand over her mouth, smothering her. She felt a cold strap laid over her stomach and then a quick, vicious tug. They took her hands and fastened them down. Her legs were free and, not knowing what else to do, she kicked out wildly. She was still kicking wildly when suddenly a tremendous weight descended upon her. The room went dark. . . .

When she opened her eyes there was the taste of brandy in her mouth. Again she kicked out and again the weight descended upon her . . . again, again, and again . . . as if a regiment were passing through the room.

When she came to again she was lying in the gutter, at the

waterfront. She screamed at the top of her lungs—but nobody came. Louder and louder she screamed. Finally footsteps sounded and then a club dropped and made a banging, droning noise. Once more the darkness enveloped her and then there were buttons gleaming and a man bending over her. His breath was foul and in his eyes green bottles danced and then the wheels rolled again with a grinding noise and joggled her and her spine cracked and she begged them not to grind her to pieces. They carried her into a dark room. It was cold and she felt her stockings slipping down. Shadows swooped down from the bulging walls and a soft, spongy hand that smelled of Lysol fastened itself over her mouth. She tried to struggle, but her limbs were caught in a vise and the vise was made of ice and there were tons of it weighing her down, searing her burning flesh. After a time the shadows disappeared and she struggled, fiercely and quietly this time, to free herself. Pains shot through her loins, her muscles were twisted into knots, and her spine—her spine felt as if it had been cracked with an ax. She waited for someone to come and pour brandy down her throat, to pick her up and toss her again. But no one came.

She was in a dream. She dreamed that she had imagined it all. But when she awoke she was still pinned down and there were people standing about her bed, men and women with evil faces and deaf ears. They massed together, shifted from side to side, moved toward her as if to fall on her and then faded away; they circled above her head like angels, rested on her bosom with their fat behinds; they fell away and added up again, like a column of figures. "Be quiet!" they said. "Shut up!" When she tried to push them away she couldn't move her limbs. She was paralyzed.

For hours and hours no one came and the walls remained solid and white and nothing changed. The monotony of it was driving her mad; she knew that she was mad because when you are not mad things happen, the walls have doors and they open, there is sunlight and fragrance and people passing and voices and you can move your hands. . . . Later, much later—weeks, it seemed—the faces reappeared. They were different now—more kindly, and not so deaf. They unloosened her straps and they touched her gently. Angels they were, but crazy, crazy angels. She asked for water and they recited from *Zarathustra*. And while they were reciting suddenly there rose a queer, cracked voice singing off-key, singing like a ventriloquist drinking a glass of water. The angels began to sing, too. They sang in unison and rolled their eyes lasciviously. Even when they had gone the singing still continued—at first high up toward the ceiling, then directly beneath her bed. It sounded as if they were singing in the chamber pot and the chamber pot cracked. Always the same cracked tune, always the same greasy words . . . over and over, as if a Victrola stuffed away in the belly of an automaton were running down.

Part 3

Part 3

1

THE NIGHT came on and he fled before his thoughts. Hildred had been in with Vanya, and then they had gone, or rather, they had fled, after a shameful scene concluded with curses and threats of violence.

He wandered dismally from one sordid memory to another. Time went by but he made no movement; his breast was empty, his limbs composed as if already he had made the final gesture, had dropped off into deep and everlasting sleep. Was it like this, then, at the end, when the eyes stared round and glassy and all the sounds of the earth fell away?

The shadows of the night stretched out and flattened against the wall with somber fantasticality. He riveted upon them his large, dolorous eyes, and behold, they trembled and all the room began to dance lightly. A rush of familiar phrases came to his lips—*a good name is better than precious ointment, and the day of death than the day of one's birth. . . . the dead know not anything, neither have they any more a reward; for the memory of them is forgotten.* He thought of Bob Ingersoll standing at the tomb of Napoleon with a torrent of words on his lips; he thought of all the infidels who had recanted on their deathbed and a voice sounded in his ears, saying: *"How dieth the wise man? As the fool."*

The phrases leaped from his brain in a confused cloud, as if all the mornings of all the Sundays he had spent in church were united in a tangled dream, nothing of which remained but a loud Presbyterian voice spewing the cruds of hoary grace. An odor of bay rum filled his nostrils and he felt again a wiry mustache pressed against his lips. A voice, honeyed and ingratiating, whispered to him, but he would not look, for the sight of the old man's throat was like an open sepulcher.

He stood before the open window and exposed himself to the shivering blasts. It was winter and everything was dead. A deep, painless sleep. In the yard there was a gaunt, bare tree. It would be droll, he thought, if in the morning when Hildred went to the window she would see his frozen body fastened like a curse against the sky. But in the morning what would it matter how they found him, or where? By morning he would have joined all the mornings that ever were.

He went to bed and pulled the covers over him. A numbness spread through his limbs; he began to glow, to burn. Were there minutes allotted him, or only seconds? At least he ought to leave a message—one always left a message at the end. He jumped out of bed again and searched feverishly for pencil and paper.

The words raced along as if driven by a lash, staining the smooth, white surface in a continuous, erratic line. As he finished, a cold dank breath that savored already of the grave passed over him. The pencil dropped from his hand, and as the heavy lids fell over his eyes he was rapt away into another time, into a world without end, a frozen void that twanged to the doleful notes of an iron harp.

Over the frozen rim of the void there rose a fiery ball raining rivers of scarlet. He knew now that the end had come, that from this livid, smoldering circle of doom there was no retreat. He was on his knees, his head buried in the black scum. Suddenly a hand seized him by the nape of the neck and flung him backward into the mire. His arms were pinioned. Above him, digging her bony knees into his chest, was a naked hag. She kissed him with her soiled lips and her breath was hot as a bride's. He felt her bony arms tightening about him, pressing him to her loins. Her loins grew big and soft, her belly white and full; she lay against him like a heavy blossom, the petals of her mouth parted lasciviously. Suddenly, in her clawlike grip, there glittered a bright blade; the blade descended and the blood spurted over his neck and into his eyes. He felt his drums bursting and a flood pouring out of his mouth. She lowered her head and rubbed her scaly lips across his cheeks. Gory, she raised her face, and again the blade descended, slid along the side of his face, plunged into his throat and laid the gullet open. Swiftly and neatly she cut away the lobes of his ears. The sky was one great river of scarlet churning with swans and silver whales; a hollow, mocking twang filled the void and the swans flew down, their long necks vibrating like taut strings. . . .

THERE WAS a bang and the door flew open. He heard his name. He turned and sighed deeply.

Hildred threw herself on the bed. "Tony, what have you done?" She gathered him in her arms and rocked him, rocked him to and fro. Like a river drowning in the sea it was. They were one again, as they had always been, as they would be forever more. Nothing, no not anything, could ever separate them again.

And then there came a loud knock at the door. Hildred trembled, twitched in his grasp. "Lie still!" he whispered, and tightened his arms about her. Again the knock, louder this time, imperative, threatening.

Vanya enters . . . à la Modjeska. Surveys the scene with cool comprehending glance. Stands beside the bed and regards the prostrate figure as if it were an ikon of our Lord Immanuel. She speaks to Hildred in a low, intimate voice, and as she speaks she slowly raises her eyes from the bed and focuses them on some invisible object far and beyond the walls.

Solicitously Hildred bends over him. "Vanya wants to know if she can do something for you," she says.

He pulls her close. "Tell her to go," he whispers.

Hildred pulls herself up and looks at Vanya confusedly. "He wants to rest," she says. "That's it, Tony, lie back and rest. We'll leave you for a little while. We'll be back soon."

Vanya had already slipped out. She was descending the stairs.

"You'll come back alone?" he said.

"Yes, I'll come back alone," Hildred answered.

"Then, take this," he said, stuffing the crumpled pages into her hand.

2

EXACTLY TWO and a half hours later, Hildred returned—with Vanya. They were radiantly happy. They hummed softly as they flitted about the room. They came and sat on the edge of the bed and attended him like ministering angels.

"Why do you look so miserable?" said Hildred. "We didn't mean to stay so long."

"The time just flew," said Vanya, gazing straight ahead of her with that far-off expression and the cocoons in her eyes.

"I wish you would sit still," he said, "and not talk."

"You're nervous," said Hildred, and then she remembered suddenly that she was to have brought something back with her.

WHEN THEY were gone some time he got out of bed, closed the windows, and quietly proceeded to dress himself. On the bureau, where she had thrown it carelessly when she returned, lay Hildred's bag. The pages he had given her were sticking out of the bag, a little more crumpled than before. He took them and smoothed them out, and as he did so, he noticed that they were not in order, neither were they in the disorder which might follow upon a hasty reading. He spread them out and examined them closely. He followed the mark of her thumb—there were food stains here and there and one of them had been burned by a cigarette. But some had not been touched at all.

It was clear to him now how the time had flown. They were so hungry that they had gone to the restaurant and gorged themselves. While waiting for the food, Vanya no doubt had suggested glancing over the letter. The letter? Why Hildred had almost forgotten about it. They read it together, and Vanya tilted back in her chair and blew smoke rings while Hildred waded through the soft slush. A comment now and then—"I really think you love him!" or "What does he mean when he calls you his vulture?" Etc. And then the waiter arrived with the food and the letter was placed to one side and a little soup was spilled on it. And the waiter smiled probably as he read a few lines over Hildred's shoulder. And after they had laughed and chatted, made plans for the morrow, or perhaps for the night itself, the coffee came along. The butts piled up in the swimming saucers. And then, no doubt, they stuck their elbows on the table and leaned forward to talk brilliantly, because when they struck a pose like this the eyes of everybody in the restaurant were fastened on them. They probably admitted to each other that they were unique in the world, and the world a sordid, stupid place. And as they prattled on thus their elbows dug deeper into the table and the time flew and they were very happy sitting there together and their bellies were full.

He closed his eyes as if to bring back more vividly the scene he imagined. Now and then his lips moved. Clearly he saw it all, directed their movements and their speech. Just as a play can be more real than reality so he was able to interpret for them what they were unable to interpret for themselves. Every detail stood out in a blinding, scorching light. Even to the last gesture when Hildred, swinging through the revolving door, a laugh on her lips, suddenly remembered that she was to bring something back with her. Yes, and the waiter running up in his greasy jacket, flourishing the crumpled pages. . . .

THEY WERE running up the steps, stumbling in their haste. He remarked the astonishment on their faces when they saw him standing there, fully dressed, the letter crumpled in his fist. The next moment he heard a heavy thumping on the stairs and then a burly fellow appeared in the doorway sliding a trunk over the thick carpet.

He looked from one to the other frowningly.

"It's my trunk," said Vanya, giggling.

He went up to Hildred, his voice quivering with rage. "What did I say about that trunk?"

Says Hildred: "Oh, this is no time to . . ."

"Get that goddamned thing out of here!"

"But Tony . . ."

"Don't Tony me! Get it out . . . quick!"

Says Vanya: "But we haven't any money left, we can't take it back."

"Oh, you can't? Well, I'll show you." He dragged it to the hallway, balanced it a moment at the top of the stairs, then gave it a push. There was a splintering crash. A door was flung open and a woman rushed out screaming.

"He's going mad!" cried Hildred, and she rushed down the stairs pulling Vanya after her.

73

Part 4

Part 4

1

———◆———

THE NEW home was large and gloomy. It had been a laundry once. From the crude fixtures in the ceiling hung pieces of twine which brushed against one's brow. A pale, wan light trickled in through the burlap curtains. Hildred hated the sunlight.

In the outhouse was a huge iron sink where the dirty dishes accumulated. The only source of heat was an open fireplace which was out of order. No one had thought to inquire about a gas range or to observe whether there were clothes closets, etc. Despite the drawbacks, Hildred and Vanya declared it to be a jolly place. It was the sort of den that appealed to their bohemian natures.

As soon as they had received permission they commenced redecorating the rooms. The green walls were converted to pitchblende, the ceiling ripened into a violet shudder, the electric bulbs were tinted a Venetian pink and etched with obscene designs. Then came the frescoes. Vanya began with her own room first. It was a little cell separated from the lavatory by a barred window. Directly above her cot a toilet box was suspended. The faint, gurgling tinkle of the drains soothed her nerves.

While she worked the two Danish sisters who owned the house looked on with prurient eyes. They would bring down liverwurst sandwiches and beer, and when they got better acquainted, they finally produced long black cigars which they smoked leisurely and with deep contentment. Vanya was not long in acquiring the habit. Hildred was the only one to demur; she said the cigars were vile. They probably were.

One day Vanya plucked up courage to ask the sisters to pose for her. They were flattered at first, but when it dawned on them that they were to pose in the nude, they reneged. After a little persuasion, however, they consented—not in the altogether, but in chemise and hose. And so, day after day, they stood shivering with cigars in their mouths, their bodies composed in the suggestive order of a bacchanal. Just as a Chinese artist will faithfully reproduce a broken plate, so Vanya reproduced these hungry madonnas—she verified every wrinkle, every crease, every wart.

The walls of the ménage soon began to heave, to scream and dance. Vanya's inventiveness was inexhaustible. At the far end, adjacent to the outhouse, a circus of toppling skyscrapers opened the legend; in the open spaces, on velvet greenswards, the weary megalopolitans could be seen pursuing their degenerate practices. From this Sodom it was but a jump to the Gomorrah of Paris—Paris with its kiosks and urinals, its quays and bridges, its fizzing boulevards and zinc bars. Looking at a narrow panel beneath the word "Montparnasse," one had the sensation of standing inside a *urinoir* plastered with municipal proclamations. A tableau of figures, one below the other, presented vividly to the imagination the dire effects of venereal infection. To make the circuit of the rooms was to receive a painful crosscut of our civilization:

there was the machine, the ghetto, the palatial lobbies of the money-grubbers, the speakeasy, the funny paper, the dance halls, the insane asylums—all fused into a maelstrom of color and rhythm. And, as if this were not enough, a special area was given over to the *fantastique*. Here Vanya permitted herself the liberty of painting her unconscious. Here flowers grew with stupendous human organs; here monsters rose up out of the deep, their jaws dripping with slime, and united shamelessly; from the facades of cathedrals huge teats, bursting with milk, swelled out; children instructed the aged, their belts slung with Korans and Talmuds; words unprintable floated in a sky drunk with blood through which zeppelins sailed upside down, piloted by such queer fellows as Pythagoras and Walther von der Vogelweide; sea cows mooched along side by side with amberjacks, and painted sunsets with their tails.

Tony Bring looked on incredulously, applauded, or put in a suggestion now and then, marveling all the while at the fecundity of this genius with the dirty fingernails.

Alone, he fell into his usual vegetal ruminations, or wandered moodily from one room to another, surveying the walls absentmindedly. When Hildred returned (she was still at the Caravan) he would sit before her like a frozen clam. He was like a cipher which they erased or not, as they pleased. If he got in the way they bumped him, set him going like a pendulum. A pendulum! Something that ticked off their comings and goings. Every day the situation grew more and more cockeyed. Especially when Hildred was around. She would commence in the middle of a sentence or ask him to set the alarm when he picked up a book. She wanted them to argue with her, to gush, to rhapsodize. She wanted to sparkle, not to chew. Words . . . words . . . words. . . . She gobbled them up, spewed them out again, added them up, juggled them, nursed them along, carried them to bed and put them under the pillow like soiled pajamas, slept on them, snored over them. Words. . . . When every other memory of her had fled there would remain—HER WORDS.

HOURS AHEAD of time, like a clock that's been advanced, he would commence to remind them that it was time to go to bed. Toward five o'clock, when the trucks began to rumble by and there came the familiar clip-clop of the milkman's horse, they would at last make preparations to retire. And then, when he had gotten into bed with Hildred, just as they were dozing off, Vanya would start prowling through the hall, muttering to herself. Sometimes she would knock at their door and get Hildred out of bed in order to hold a whispered conversation in the zenana.

And what did they talk about in there? Always the same rigmarole: Vanya was morbid. . . . Vanya had received bad news from home. . . . Vanya had been thinking again about the insane asylum. Sometimes it was nothing more than a fit of depression due to a bad start she had made with a canvas.

"Look here," he said one night, as they lay fondling each other, "am I never to have an evening with you alone? Must I always share you with her?"

"But you're not *sharing* me," said Hildred, cuddling up to him affectionately.

He suggested that they go somewhere together the next evening, to which Hildred immediately replied that it was out of the question. For one thing, she couldn't afford to take a night off.

"But when you're through . . . ?"

"I'll see," said Hildred. "But not tomorrow, at any rate. Tomorrow I have an appointment with someone."

These appointments meant money. No way of rebutting that argument.

Oddly enough, the appointment didn't prove important enough to keep. Something else, something of a more important nature, had intervened. Quite spontaneously . . . quite unexpectedly, of course. One of her old customers had dropped in at the dinner hour and offered Hildred a couple of theater tickets which would otherwise have gone to waste.

It was remarkable, moreover, how everyone remembered to bring her violets. At the appropriate moment he brought up the subject of the violets. But he was mistaken again—as he usually was. The man hadn't brought her the violets—he hadn't even taken her to the theater. It was Vanya who went to the theater with her.

"But who gave you the violets then?"

"Someone else."

"To be sure, but who?"

"Who? Why, the Spaniard." She said it as if he knew all about the Spaniard, whereas he had never heard of him before. But he must have been mistaken about that, too, because most of the time he didn't pay any attention to what she was telling him.

The story of the violets had an almost plausible ring. There were always plenty of boobs dropping in to hand her flowers. One day, however, after an unusual to-do about the subject (it was one of his bad habits to open up old sores), he decided to have a little chat with the florist whose shop was just around the corner from the Caravan.

It was a Greek who ran the shop. Tony Bring dropped in

and asked quite casually to see the violets which the two young ladies usually ordered of him. The Greek shrugged his shoulders. Which two young ladies? There were lots of young ladies who bought violets.

Tony Bring described them—the long mane, the bare legs, the green face.

"Oh, those two! Sure . . . sure. Here, thees is eet!"

A few hours later he went back and bought a bunch. He felt foolish walking along with a bouquet in his hand. He felt still more ridiculous when he stepped into the Caravan and presented them. It was the dinner hour and the place was jammed. Hildred had spotted him immediately; she had rushed up to him and squeezed his hand. She took him by the arm and ushered him outside. They stood in the little yard fenced in by the iron railing.

He had two seats in his pocket for *Potemkin*. She was going to make an effort to get away, to give him an evening, as he had requested. He walked around the block a few times, as she had suggested. When she came out again he was met with a sorrowful look. "I can't get away," she said. "We're short of girls tonight."

"But can't you take sick suddenly?"

Nope. They were on to that game.

He walked off dejectedly. At the corner he turned around. She was waving to him. She seemed to be genuinely disappointed, and yet she was smiling, too.

He stood outside the lobby of the theater and watched the crowds pouring in. It was like a Zionist reunion. No one seemed to come alone. He saw a young couple, shabbily dressed, advancing eagerly toward the box office. He went up to them and offered them his tickets. As they were mumbling their thanks he turned his back and made off. He was swallowed up by the crowd and borne along at a ridiculous pace. They moved like an army of ants pushing through a crack in the sidewalk. As he drifted with the current, shunted here and there, rudderless, will-less, like a straw riding a whirlpool, he suddenly made up his mind to go back to the Caravan—no particular reason, just a blind impulse.

Anchoring himself at the railing he gazed through the window. He saw the girls weaving in and out among the tables with the huge trays balanced in midair, stopping now and then to chat with some fresh Alec who knew how to put his arm around a girl's waist or pinch her buttocks. But there was no sign of Hildred. He went inside and inquired for her. They said she had gone off.

It was a strange coincidence, as things turned out. Hildred did go to see *Potemkin* after all. That very night. The Spaniard had hopped in—at the last minute—just when one of the girls who had been away ill returned for duty. And, strange as it may seem, he too had tickets for *Potemkin*. Extraordinary it was. Perfectly extraordinary. That's how things happened in life. And, of course, there was no sense in refusing him. Besides, hadn't she gone with the hope of seeing him somewhere in the audience?

But when he admitted that he didn't go she seemed amazed. "You didn't go?" she repeated. She couldn't understand. "Why, it was a marvelous picture! Marvelous! The way those Cossacks descended the stairs leading to the quay, the way they halted, like automatons, and fired into the mob. And the way that mob melted!" She described most vividly how a baby carriage had rolled down the long, white steps, how they dropped, the women and children, how they were trampled on. It was magnificent. What gorgeous beasts those Cossacks were!

She left off abruptly, lit herself a cigarette, and sat on the edge of the table, swinging her leg.

"Do you know what a real pogrom is like?" she asked suddenly.

He knew that the answer to this was no. He said no.

She thought as much. He ought to hear Vanya talk. Vanya had taken part in more than one pogrom. . . .

"Where?" he demanded.

In Russia, to be sure. Where did he suppose?

"She's a Russian, then?"

She was not only a Russian, he learned, but she was a princess, a Romanoff, a bastard Romanoff. So that's how it was! Not only a genius, but a princess to boot. He couldn't help but think of another Romanoff who had once given him a bad check for three dollars. He was a genius, too, in a way . . . and a bastard, to boot. He wagged his head, like a Jew who has just been informed of a fresh calamity. No wonder he was not romantic enough for them; he was neither a genius, nor a Romanoff, nor a bastard.

The scene came to a termination on the bed. It was marvelous the way Hildred could pour out her love. The man who could doubt such a love was an idiot. Body and soul she gave herself. A complete surrender. Not like those half-women in the Village, whom Willie Hyslop consorted with, but like a real woman with all her organs intact, all her senses unstrung, all her heart on fire and her passions burning to cinder . . . a veritable pogrom of love.

At the very climax Vanya had to return.

"Oh, you're *there*!" she cried. She could smell them in the dark, like a dog.

No sooner than she heard her voice Hildred jumped out of bed. The princess had arrived. Time to sing another tune. Tony Bring slipped out the back door into the outhouse. The dirty dishes were lying in the sink. He moved about aimlessly, glancing through the window now and then to see if they took any notice of his absence. No, they seemed not to notice anything. Hildred was cold-creaming her face while the princess sang to her. They sang in English, in German, in French, in Russian. Vanya went to her room and came back with her Barrymore makeup. Swagger and strut. Hildred sitting by, like an empress of emotion, doling out applause.

The roof of the outhouse was supported by three iron poles. Tony Bring raced around the poles like an electrified rabbit. Each time he passed the window he glanced inside. They were still singing . . . caroling away like a couple of drunken molls. "Let me call you sweetheart, I'm in love with you-ou-ou . . ." Over and over they sang it. George Washington should have been there—and Abraham Lincoln and Jean Cocteau and Puvis de Chavannes and Moholy-Nagy and Tristan Tzara. . . . He was there and he was not there. He was like a ghost at a banquet, like a hero without a medal, like an uninvited guest at a wake, like a slack-wire walker without a bamboo pole or an umbrella. He was a lunatic at large with a chronometer hidden in his socks. There was a transparent window but he was invisible to them. If they couldn't see him they could at least hear him thrashing about like a maniac, or couldn't they? Were they deaf, too? Yes, they were deaf. They were deafening themselves with song and laughter. The world was empty but for them. Their song filled the world, filled the starry space beyond, made the stars and planets hum and the moon drunk and the heavens to sing.

"You bloody devils!" he groaned. "If I only knew the way

to sink my hooks into you! If I could only teach you to dance a few steps!"

This night, sure as hellfire, there will be a poem—a poem about the veils of night, about the hours grinding and hacking away at space with their sandy arms. O earth! thou art a breathing tomb, a chamber to torture these living dead with their widespread guts and their hidebound hands gaping to heaven for succor. In that frowsy cubicle where the Danish sisters bulge from the wall the pen will soon be scratching feverishly. Through the drunken verses they will reel and totter and the room will be split with grunts and squeals. While the music gurgles from the drains and spiders crawl over their black stockings the pen will dance. . . . Take away these cadavers that are growing in my brain! Give me back my soul and the sockets of my eyes!

2

THE CARAVAN has added another hostess to its staff: one of the Romanoff family! God, if people only realized that they were being served by a princess! The way she poured the soup! The way she balanced the tray!

Princesses have a way of being disappointing, but this one . . . ! Not a full-blooded princess, of course. Somewhere there had been a little slip. Somebody had hitched his horse to the wrong post—during a pogrom or a snowstorm.

Hildred felt like another person. She jerked Vanya out of bed more tenderly. A princess was such a delicate thing. Arm in arm they left the house each day. They returned when it suited them.

When they are gone Tony Bring closets himself in the sanctuary left vacant by the princess. He reviews what her alter ego has lucubrated during the night, for between two and six in the morning it is not a Romanoff but a Madame Villon who inhabits the holy of holies. Madame Villon writes in a childish scrawl, as if she had been mesmerized. Not having a slate she writes on matchboxes, on menus and blotters; sometimes nothing will do but toilet paper. Having written, she tosses her poems on the floor. Walks off in the morning like a dog leaving its dung.

This morning, fresh from the griddle, Tony Bring finds a hymn to ammonia. "You held yourself like a fallen queen . . . your eyes, three eyes, spirits of ammonia." It was written on the back of a menu from Lenox Avenue. "Swaying chalk arms blacked with life passed over my eyes. . . . I looked to you, Hildred, through the weaving green lights, and I wondered. . . . You were drunk last night, Hildred."

Last night! That was the night Vanya came home raving about the Spaniard's wasted skull floating in a sea of navels, glossy brown navels smudged with lip rouge. That was the night they were to raise the rent money and there were violets again and the Spaniard had said jokingly, "Someday I weel keel her!" He read on. . . . "Thick gold chains clinked in my brain, the music roared in a trickling flood over my ginger ale. The floor is rocking, the ice water is freezing my ankles."

HE SWOOPED down on the Caravan at dinner hour. The ceremony with which he was received embarrassed him. They insisted on waiting on him together. Such deference they paid him! One would think he was a celebrity who had chosen to dine in this humble place for the express purpose of shedding over these two devoted creatures the aura of his august personage. They even went through the farce of creating a little scene, pretended to be jealous of each other because he was distributing his favors unevenly.

He deliberately prolonged his stay. Already Hildred was betraying evidences of impatience, though with admirable and unwonted restraint. It was obvious that there were plans afoot for the evening. They were simply marking time.

He lingered over the dessert, ordered a second cup of coffee, fiddled around with his notebook, jotted down a few meaningless phrases. Hildred was on the verge of exasperation. She sat down beside him and began to plead with him to go. Vanya stood behind her, taking in every word, yet managing somehow to preserve a dreamy, rapt expression as if it were all of no consequence to her.

"Don't you think it's silly," Hildred was saying, "to come here and spy on me? Do you think you'll learn anything by hanging on here?"

"But I haven't come to spy on you," he said. "I've come to take you out."

Hildred frowned, then shot a quick glance at Vanya that said: "For Christ's sake, get me out of this!"

But to the amazement of both of them Vanya responded promptly: "He's right, Hildred . . . I think it's your duty to go with him tonight."

"But we had an appointment. . . ."

"Oh, I'll take care of that," said Vanya. "Forget about it."

"Can't you come along with us?" said Hildred, a sulky, pouty look on her face.

No, Vanya couldn't. She was resolute about it. Moreover, she simply couldn't bring herself to intrude upon their pleasure. She spoke so sincerely that for a moment Tony Bring actually felt grateful to her. Meanwhile his resentment toward Hildred was growing to such proportions that it was only by summoning all his powers of will that he managed to persuade himself to see the thing through. He wondered what fresh excuses would rise to her lips. And, at the same time, there grew in him a stronger and stronger determination to impose his will.

Finally, after she had gulped down a cup of black coffee

and lit a fresh cigarette, Hildred gave in. At the door she pulled Vanya aside. A prolonged, agitated conversation went on in whispers. At the conclusion of it Vanya was beaming.

The very way she held her cigarette, the way she puffed at it silently, vengefully, galled him. He had a mad desire to tear it from her mouth, to fling it in the gutter. The next moment, however, he found himself searching feverishly for some word that would dissolve this feud, some gesture that would bring her close to him.

"Well?" Her voice sang out with renewed insolence. "Where are we going?"

They were standing outside the subway entrance to Sheridan Square. Opposite was the cafeteria frequented by the Village freaks. It was in the show window here that Willie Hyslop sometimes sat, looking for all the world like John the Baptist.

"You're not taking me *there*, I hope?" she said, observing the direction of his glance.

Savagely he grasped her arm and pulled her down the steps.

THEY WERE in a Chinese garden, an orchestra playing softly in a rose-colored light, lovers voluptuously squeezed into a tiny rectangle roped off by heavy velvet cords strung through shiny brass posts. The expression on Hildred's face which had irritated him so only a while ago had disappeared completely. It was almost gratitude that showed itself now. She looked at once for the little booth on the Broadway side where the huge electric sign blazed. It was here they had come to know each other, here in this very booth that she had begun to build up that fiction about herself which she clung to still, which she elaborated, in fact, as time went on. They trembled as their knees touched. When the music started up and they heard again that melody which had once run through their veins like liquid fire the tears came to their eyes. Arm in arm they moved toward the floor where, in the tiny rose-colored rectangle, the amorous and the bewitched were voluptuously squeezed together. Clasping each other in a warm embrace, they floated blissfully with the others, everything forgotten now except the memory of that night when they had come together and had remained together for days without end. It was like a fragment of a dream which, by an effort scarcely calculable, is revived again and again in the fraction of a second, is revived without a change, vivid, naked, complete. Softly she sang the words in his ear; the touch of her cheek like a burn, her voice a drug, her breasts, soft and full, swelling with the melody. It was a song that Vanya had never heard—he marked that well. If the day ever came . . . He checked himself. Why should he think of that? Why not drink, drink to the full from this cup of happiness?

Seated at the table they exchanged pensive glances. Was she too thinking of all that had come between them? Was she too thinking of that bliss which they had sworn could never be destroyed? Or was that faraway look in her eyes born of some sudden remembrance . . . the last few words with Vanya . . . that whispered consultation at the door of the Caravan? His gaze rested on her lips and hung there timidly. The least word about Vanya now and the spell would be broken. . . .

No, thank God, her first words were not cruel. Little words

they were, of no account, but laden with reminders of a distant enchantment. He watched her lips closely, her mouth so soft and promising, her tongue that seemed to caress each word as if it were flesh fragrant and yearning. Her smile was like the sun coming out after a shower, like the sun beaming upon a strange and lovely city. There flashed through his mind a vision of Paris, of its colored walls, its gray skies that changed from milk to pearl, the wet green of the gardens, the reflections in the Seine. . . . He looked at her intently, steadfastly. One could hardly call it a smile, this weird, supernatural glow. The flame burned too steadily, the features remained illuminated, like a statue leaping out of the altarplace when darkness envelops the church.

Paris! His head was full of Paris. In the last few days they had been singing nothing but Paris, Paris, Paris. . . . What memories the name evoked! Sundays on the butte at Montmartre, picnics in the Bois de Boulogne, the carousels in the Tuileries, the lake in the Luxembourg where the youngsters sailed their boats. He thought of the lovers who pressed against each other in the Métro, the lovers who embraced in public, in the parks, on the streets, everywhere. Christ, how they made love in Paris! And the twilight hour—that eerie, metallic glow in the sky, as if it were a piece of metal played on by vivid lights, streaked with hasty daubs by an enormous, unseen hand. A different sky altogether, the Paris sky. A northern sky.

Held now by the fanatical brilliance of her eyes, he felt again the sensual, tangible beauty of soft-black roofs that glistened in the sun after a warm rain. The most beautiful tones of black there were in these roofs—like certain warm, utterly indescribable values of charcoal.

As the evening wore on it seemed impossible that his cup of happiness could hold another drop.

And then a wretched, a most disagreeable thing occurred. As she was fumbling for change to hand the waiter, an envelope dropped from Hildred's bag. She looked at it with a start, was about to snatch it up when, observing that he made no attempt to intercept her, she suddenly altered her decision and allowed the envelope to remain where it had fallen, exposed to full view.

Tony Bring recognized the childish scrawl at once. "Let me read it," he was about to say, but Hildred had already closed her hand over it and was stuffing it away in her bag. The panic and the fear expressed by this gesture sickened him.

"Believe me," said Hildred, "I can't let you see it.... I really can't, I have no right to."

Never in her life had she spoken more sincerely, more earnestly.

"It has nothing to do with us at all," she said. "Not a thing!" She used the word *sacred*. There was something in the letter which was *sacred* to Vanya, which she couldn't reveal even to him. A struggle went on in him; now, more than ever, he wanted to believe in her. It was imperative to believe in her, he told himself. She was a liar, that he knew, that he forgave; but this was not a question of a lie. Again, as when he had waited for her in the furnished room overlooking the harbor, he had a sense of impending evil, a wild, uncontrollable fear that everything would be taken from him. Nevertheless, he allowed the incident to pass over; he said not another word about the letter.

On the way home Hildred's tongue wagged incessantly. She seemed to have lost control of herself. She didn't seem to

93

care what she said; it was as though she were trying to drown the incident. But the more she opened the dikes the higher it rose; it floated there on the ocean of her words like a cork that will not be submerged.

"You say you love us both?" he interrupted, breaking the long silence he had maintained.

"Yes," said Hildred, "I love you both, though my love for you is different than my love for Vanya."

"Think what you are saying, Hildred!" he said. There was neither hostility nor irritation in his voice; he had that feeling of calm, mingled with a profound curiosity, which comes to us at times in moments of great danger. "Think, Hildred, is it love you have for her? People don't use the word *love* as loosely as all that. . . ."

But Hildred wasn't in the least deflected by this. Though she didn't quite know how to put it, there was this much to it, she wanted him to know: men were different. It was impossible to compare the affection between two men and the affection which might exist between two women. With women it was something normal, spontaneous, and in full accord with their instincts. But when a man avowed his love for another man it was unnatural. She amended this by saying that there had been cases, to be sure, where men loved each other in a purely Platonic way.

Platonic! It was one of those words which had been bandied about frequently during their nightly discussions, one of the words which were underlined with a red pencil.

"Listen," she said, "could I lie in your arms and give myself to you the way I do if . . . ?"

"If what?"

"Oh, this is all so stupid! You make things complex,

you make them ugly. You do! You see things only in your narrow, masculine way. You make everything a matter of sex, and it isn't that at all . . . it's something rare and beautiful."

This thought carried her away. "And then to think," she added, "that you harbor all these nasty thoughts about me when I have nothing in me but love for you . . . love and gratitude . . . because I owe everything to you, I was nothing at all, just a silly child, and you made something of me. You're almost a god to me, don't you know that, don't you believe me?"

IT WAS very late when they got home, and Vanya had apparently retired. They were amazed, when they turned on the lights, to observe the transformation that had been wrought in their absence. The place had been dusted, the floor polished, the furniture neatly arranged. The table in the middle room was covered with a piece of tapestry, and in the center of it stood a vase filled with gardenias. They noticed, too, that the light above the table had been fitted with a shade, one of those parchment affairs on which the map of the ancient world is stamped.

"You see!" Hildred exclaimed. "You see how thoughtful she can be?" She lounged through the rooms, examining everything carefully, giving vent at the same time to eager murmurs, extreme and rapturously prolonged.

As for Tony Bring, his enthusiasm was tepid. In the first place, it was so obviously a gesture, to use one of Vanya's own expressions; secondly, as often as he had performed this task himself (not with quite this finesse, admittedly) there had never been even the slightest reverberation of approval, or of thanks. Never before had Vanya given a thought to straightening the house; the dishes might lie in the sink for a week, for all it mattered to her. She didn't even bother to pick up her clothes when they fell on the floor. It was so much easier to step over things.

Hildred was unable to restrain her thanksgiving until the morning. "I must go in and see if she is awake," she said.

Gently he tried to hold her back. "Please, Hildred, not tonight. . . . Tonight you . . ." And he finished it by catching her up in a passionate embrace.

"But just let me see if she's awake. I'll be right back."

The moment he relaxed his hold she slipped out of his grasp. Instead of going directly to Vanya's room she flew to the bathroom.

His thoughts traveled at top speed. He strode back and forth, or stood stock-still in front of Vanya's sea cows and looked straight through them without even noticing the sun-sets they were painting with their tails. Mechanically he pulled up a chair, straddled it, his arms resting on its back, his head hanging down loosely, ready to roll off. The floor was spotless, it shone like a pair of patent-leather boots. Vanya had done this. She had gotten down on her hands and knees. Vanya. . . .

There was a window in the bathroom and the window was barred. They were probably talking through the bars, talking rapidly because soon the warden would come and the visitor would have to leave. Then she would be alone again in her little cell, the cell with the wooden box from which the music gurgled. And the pen would hiss and scratch again, flies walking upside down, sandy arms hacking away at space,

give me back the sockets in my eyes. . . . He raised his head
for a moment and he saw a urinal plastered with warnings
against venereal infection. He thought of the Chinese garden
and the song she had sung in his ear, and the conversation
later over the syrupy black coffee. The spoons were very dull
. . . washed too many times. And as he recalled the dull hue
of the spoons and what she had said about the love between
man and man he noticed her bag lying there on the table. It
had been lying there all the time, almost within his grasp. She
must have laid it there when she came in, flung it down
without thinking in order to dance about the house admiring
Vanya's loving industry.

He opened it and rummaged through it quickly. He
dumped the contents on the table and searched and
searched. It was gone. He looked under the table. No letter
there. He went to the bed and felt in the pockets of her cape,
looked under the pillows. It was gone.

It was not just amazement or disappointment that showed
on his face—he was shocked . . . profoundly shocked. He
spoke to himself quietly, as if he were talking in his sleep. . . .
After the wonderful way she spoke to me . . . almost a god . . .
worship you . . . but just the same she had remembered to
remove it from her bag, to hide it somewhere. He recalled
how she had stuffed it away, frantically, it seemed. He remembered it vividly. And after that not another word had
passed between them about the letter. . . .

A moment or two later Hildred returned. She was smiling
tenderly, her face as beautiful and innocent as a child's.

"And now," she said, approaching closely and offering
herself like a rare sacrifice, "my great big lover wants to . . ."
She offered him her warm lips, her heavy, tropical breasts;

her hands fell to her sides and she hung there in his arms, limp and warm.

As he carried her to the bed he thought to himself, What now? What now?

"Do you remember," she said, "what you did to me that first night? Do you remember the way . . . ?" The words died out like a warm breeze. They gazed at each other silently, the blood churning with whales and swans, the room a void twanging to their broken harps. He sank his teeth into her warm lips, buried them in her throat, bit a dull red stain in her shoulder. "Ah!" she breathed, and as they separated for a moment to fire each other again the walls seemed to heave, and their breath, coming short and heavy, filled the room with a dry, withering exhalation.

She was speaking to him with that low, vibrant voice of hers, darker now, more exotic than ever. In the subdued light of the room her flesh gleamed white and milky, her torso rose and fell like a sea, and her breath coming to him with heavy fragrance invaded his senses like a narcotic. Her language had become weirdly transformed: they were not words any longer that impinged on his mind but the carnal, vital essence, the propulsive, elemental force which projects itself beyond our words and flames there at the frontiers of thought dyeing our blood and instincts. Listening to her now he recalled the distinctions with which she had embroidered her remarks on love. Her whole being seemed nothing more than a vehicle to express the omnipresence of love, body and soul were united in proclaiming it. How ridiculous, he thought, that a word like *Platonic* should ever cross her lips: it was like saying that a live wire should always be held in the naked hand. Lingeringly he bent over her, kissed her moist, fragrant mouth. Her tongue slid between his teeth, they lay there trembling and panting. She submitted to his fondling, encouraged him with low murmurs, took his hand in hers and with her burning touch directed its fugitive pursuit. And as they lay thus he questioned her—about others whom she had gone with, about the functioning of her body, about the most intimate details of her emotional life. She made no attempt to withhold anything, nor did she seek to idealize her sentiments. Naked as her flesh were the responses she made him. Nor did he ask her whether she had loved each one in turn. He asked her instead to describe her feelings, to make comparisons, to give him the fullest picture of her desires, her thoughts, her impulses and reactions.

When in turn she questioned him he found it difficult to respond; he became so involved in his narrations that she was compelled to disbelieve him. Moreover, her sensations proved far less gratifying than she had imagined. It was easier to become roused through one's own confessions.

They grew silent again. Nothing could be heard any longer but the beating of their hearts and their breath coming heavy and irregularly. And at last that too ceased and their bodies lay prone upon the bed, inert, drugged, only the muscles twitching under the moist envelope of flesh.

3

EVERY MORNING a calliope went by in a covered wagon. Its
passage filled the house with salacious sounds. And every
morning, driven frantic by the monotony of its plaint, Vanya
leaped out of bed with an oath and fled through the rooms
like a water buffalo in pursuit of a rainbow. Hildred, tossing
in her sleep, would groan or mutter broken phrases as she
dreamed of purple hippogriffs falling through the roof. Each
morning Tony Bring bent over her and kissed her while she
twitched and tossed, and always as he studied the grave,
morbid beauty of her face hope came to him anew. How
could it be that this enchantress who the night before had
called him a god would awake to torture him afresh?

At breakfast Vanya usually chewed the cuds of her poetry.
This breakfasting was a piece of extravagance in more ways
than one. Instead of the gratuitous meal which the Caravan
offered they chose to sit in the candlelight at home and begin
the day with a brisk intellectual discussion. While Tony Bring
squeezed oranges and kept an eye on the oil stove, so that
Hildred's bacon wouldn't get too crisp, poems were shuffled
back and forth.... *Leave me a simple thing like the moon, it
is not complicated.* ... *She lay on the swaying sands whispering
to her brother of death.* ... The lines were interspersed with
parenthetical references to the coffee, or the price of strawberries.

Usually they left the house in an exuberant mood, as if they were setting forth on a holiday trip. But this morning, for some reason or other, Vanya showed no inclination to go. She talked about doing some *real* work for a change, meaning thereby a portrait of Tony Bring which she had started a few days back. Hildred, usually so eager and ready to gratify Vanya's whims, displayed a strange indifference, a hostility, one might almost call it, to this suggestion. And when Vanya added, "Jesus, it's stupid waiting on people all day . . . I'm not a horse," Hildred rose abruptly and slipping on her cape said: "Very well, amuse yourself; I'll do the dirty work." At the door she turned around and flung out: "It's fortunate I haven't any creative urge to distract me from my responsibilities—else I don't know what would become of you, the two of you."

"I didn't think she would take it like that," said Vanya, as the door slammed behind Hildred. And then impulsively: "Have you any change, Tony? I'll have to take a taxi."

But when she rushed out of the house a moment later she espied Hildred walking leisurely toward the subway. "I'm so glad you waited for me," she cried breathlessly as she caught up with her.

"I wasn't waiting at all," said Hildred. "I have a pain in my side, I can't walk any faster."

"Let's take a cab," said Vanya. It was another way of saying "Forgive me."

IT HAD been decided that Hildred was to give certain evenings to Vanya and certain evenings to her husband. And then another little matter had been brought to a conclusive termination, an event which made Tony Bring even more grateful to his spouse. That letter which had caused him so much perturbation—he never brought up the subject again but, as if to prove to him what an ass he had made of himself, Hildred had left pieces of the envelope lying on the floor near the toilet bowl. That was the way they communicated with each other on important affairs. Oh, all sorts of things were transacted that way; it was like having a secret code and a thousand times better than cheap words of explanation.

These trifles were going through Tony Bring's head as he moved about the place putting things to rights. Not so many hours ago things had looked lovely—yes, lovely. One felt the touch of a feminine hand; it brought a note of grace, of charm, into their little home. Now it was all otherwise again.

He stepped into Vanya's room. Her clothes were lying in a heap on the floor and under her cot was a mass of crumpled cigarette stubs. As he slid the broom under the cot a ten-dollar bill came to view. He might have been surprised if it had not happened before, but things like that happened every now and then. The strange part of it, however, was that money could be kicking around like this and nobody disturbed about it. Instead of being grateful to him for its recovery they behaved in the strangest manner—not quite, but *almost* as if they suspected him of filching it. But that was so silly of them, if they ever gave it a thought. Why would he be returning money to them if he had actually stolen it? And, on the other hand, short as they usually were, how was it no one ever spoke of missing a ten-dollar bill? After all, a ten-dollar bill was an item. . . .

These were part of the mysteries that continually lurked in the air. He lingered in Vanya's room to muse over a fresh batch of letters which came to light as he rummaged through the papers on her table. They were all from women—out on the Pacific coast. They addressed her as "David," "lovely Jo,"

"Michael darling," and so on. One was from a convent, from some forlorn nun whose breasts, so the letter read, hung mournfully beneath a black shroud. Another, a sweet little girl whose language indicated that she could scarcely have been more than sixteen, told how she wet the pillow each night with her tears. "Michael darling," she wrote, "don't you care for me anymore? Is there some one else—in that horrid New York—who has taken my place?" Then there was a strong, sensible letter from a woman whose husband was frightfully jealous—"He will never forgive my David," she confided in a parenthesis. This was a woman with understanding. She gave good counsel, filled her pages with loving advice, urging her "David" to concentrate all her efforts on her work. "I am not uneasy about you, dear," she concluded. "I know that you will meet other women, younger women perhaps, who will claim your friendship and enrich your days. But the nights will belong to me. I know that you are thinking of me always, that you will come back to me as soon as this madness wears off."

Underneath the letters was an unfinished note in Vanya's own hand. It was obviously a reply to this self-contained creature whose husband was so infernally jealous. "Irma, my lovely little Lesbian," he read, "these words . . . maddening, exotic, intoxicating. Your voice [here Tony Bring pondered a moment, to wonder if Hildred was in on these long-distance calls, or these adorable entreaties] . . . Christ, Irma, write to me, write often . . . tell me things. All this time—do you know what I was thinking? I thought perhaps I was another one of those Count Brugas. Oh yes, but at the same time I wrote you pages and pages, and then (you know my temperamental fits!) I tore them up. I want to say a million things but I'm shaking. Wait, I will tell things in a more repressed

103

manner. After I disappeared . . ." What followed had been mutilated and was undecipherable. On the other side it continued: "Irma, it is so wonderful to write your name. I did not succeed in committing suicide. I shall never commit suicide. [She had written "again" but crossed it out.] I love you, Irma . . . love you terribly. Have you still some of my poems? Your voice made me turn pale. I could not see you, dear, but your voice is just the same. I hear it at night when I lie in this crazy room and the walls begin to heave. Last night . . ."

Here it broke off. Two cigar stubs lay in the saucer beside the note; there was a sticky ring on the tabletop, as if a glass of liqueur had rested there. No doubt one of the Danish sisters had dropped in for a quiet little chat. The older one had grown quite fond of Vanya lately. She was behaving like a widow who goes to the cemetery to flirt over her husband's grave.

The usual palpitations which he experienced in going through Vanya's papers were strangely absent. He forgot even to shake his head in that rueful manner which was oddly characteristic of him. He read as much as his curiosity demanded—which is to say *all*—and put the pages aside. An almost cheerful grunt escaped him.

THEY RETURNED rather early that evening, the two of them. Vanya was still itching to add some touches to the portrait she had begun.

In posing it is often like sitting in the concert hall. One falls asleep, comfortably oriented, in a room in New York to wake up in an opium den in San Francisco or Shanghai. En route one murders, rapes, pulls down skyscrapers, goes skating in the tropics, feeds peanuts to yaks, or pulls a slack-wire stunt over the Brooklyn Bridge. Nor is the artist immune. Shaggy eyebrows develop into ferns, the pupil becomes a lake in which temples and swans float, the ears labyrinths dreaming of mythology.

There is a mole on Tony Bring's lower lip. Vanya has painted it a dozen times. She is obsessed by it. It is no longer a mole to her, but an arena in which there are shawls and flaming sashes, fists covered with mail, ungelded beasts. It is not a face she wants to paint—has she not painted it a thousand times in her dreams?—but this mole, this arena of her inner conflict, this froth of lust where men and beast mingle their naked passions. The mole hangs to his underlip like a verdant terrace on the brink of a precipice.

Hildred thinks how ingenious it would be if instead of doing a portrait Vanya were to create a melancholy brown horse that would fill the room with *Sehnsucht*. It is but an interlude among other thoughts which she voices as she reads aloud from *Songs of Adam*. In the Eagle Building, only a few blocks away, the great pan-democrat who sang so beautifully his goat songs hangs by a nail under a glass frame; his bushy eyebrows are smothered under a huge sombrero, his white beard stained with tobacco juice. Every day that he hangs there his songs become more apocalyptic. The grand old patriarch of American letters, friend of Horace Traubel and of car conductors, seer and homosexual, the brother of all mankind girding up his loins. . . .

Vanya throws down her brush in despair. "I can't think with all this going on!" she exclaims.

"I thought it would stimulate you," says Hildred, shutting the book with a bang.

By way of response Vanya took the canvas from the easel, and after scanning it ferociously, put her big cowhide boot through it. "I'm hungry!" she said, and in the next breath, turning to Tony Bring—"Was Walt really a homo?"

Chagrined that she should have been ignored on such an important subject, Hildred walked off to inspect the pantry. She returned with a can of sardines, a huge chunk of sour bread, some cheese and grapes. Tony Bring was talking about the poet Baudelaire, whose pathological instincts, so it was said, led him to seek out the most repulsive types of women imaginable—dwarfs, Negresses, the demented, the diseased.

"Do you want coffee or tea?" Hildred asked coldly.

"Anything," said Vanya, without looking up.

They had dubbed the table at which they sat the "gut" table. Not a very refined expression, but then neither was the language which they employed when gathered here. As a matter of fact, it had been christened thus because here, at one time or another, sometimes in turn, sometimes all together, they were given to spilling their guts. They had grown attached to the word. It was direct and full of steam—like one of Dempsey's short body blows. No kowtowing or salaaming over the gut table. No *küss die Hand* business, or *s'il vous plaît*.

"Are you or are you not a pervert?" That's how it commences around the gut table this evening.

The Bruga woman, to whom the question was addressed, doesn't always relish it in this fashion, especially with so much steam behind the punch. She attempts a little footwork, figuratively speaking—a little sidestepping and ducking. Out of luck this evening, because her assailant only closes in on her and drums a tattoo on her kidneys. And when Hildred, essaying to referee the bout, steps in between them she gets a clout for her pains.

"*You,*" he says to her, "I want to ask you a question too. Supposing," he adds rapidly and most blandly, "supposing

I'm walking through Washington Square and a man approaches me . . . solicits me. What do you think I should do—invite him to a cup of coffee or haul off and sock him one in the jaw?"

Hildred puts on a glacial stare.

"I'll put it to you a little differently," says Tony Bring hurriedly. "After all, we don't have to mince matters. I'm going to ask you what you would do if a woman—a woman like *her*, for instance—came up to you and propositioned you. . . ."

Vanya tilted back in her chair and grinned.

"Can you answer me directly and in a few words?" he shouted.

Of course Hildred couldn't. She had never said anything in a few words. Her jaws were working industriously amid the rubbish heaps of antiquity; she reeled off names and definitions and as she chewed and chewed the saliva began to flow and the tin cans and broken bottles rested more easily in her large digestive tract. She had already used up a thousand words without approaching the question.

"Get down to brass tacks!"

"But you're absurd! You go at me like a pedantic idiot."

"I'm asking you a simple, straightforward question. . . ."

"But I've told you a dozen times—I have no definite attitude. It would depend entirely on the circumstances, on the individual who approached me, on my mood, on . . ."

"You mean to say then that you don't know whether you'd be pleased or disgusted . . . is that it?"

"Disgusted?" Hildred was hedging. "After all, they're human beings just like us."

"Sure! And they're ⎯ ⎯⎯ too!"

It was an ugly term. Hildred turned white, and for the moment she was tongue-tied. But then Vanya broke in. "Not all perverts go about soliciting," she said, quite as if this were a most important detail.

"Good," he said, growing more excited, "good . . . I can get somewhere with *you*. At least you know how to talk straight."

He strode up and down several times and finally, planting himself square in front of Vanya, he said: "Will you give a frank answer to a frank question?"

The words seemed to explode in Vanya's ears. No doubt she meant, by the nod of her head, to convey her assent, but Tony Bring stood in front of her like a tormentor waiting for that word *yes* which she seemed incapable of formulating.

"Will you? Will you?" he demanded, bending forward until their noses almost touched.

Vanya's head was twitching from side to side as if she had been suddenly stricken with chorea. Her eyes were large and fixed.

Once again Hildred interposed. "I won't let her answer," she said. "You're a fool if you think you can extract things this way. If you had any intelligence you wouldn't need to ask any questions. Read your books—that's the only way you learn anything."

"Oh, is that so?" he said. They were standing close to each other, their lips curled back in a snarl, just like two mangy curs fighting over a bone. "Perhaps I don't know everything, but I know enough already to railroad her to jail. Laugh that off!"

"You fool!" cried Hildred, tossing her head defiantly. "What do you mean by that?"

"What do I mean? I mean just this—that Platonic love is

one thing and calling a woman *a darling little Lesbian* quite another. Perhaps your good friend here understands what I'm talking about." He paused a second. "Eh, Vanya, what have you to say for yourself? You know what I'm driving at. Why don't you speak?"

Vanya leaned against the wall, her hands buried in her jeans. She looked at him piercingly and with the utmost coolness and deliberation responded: "So you're convinced now that I'm a Lesbian, are you? And your wife, what is she?"

She paused just long enough for this to sink in. She was about to continue when Hildred broke in: "Exactly! If she's a Lesbian, then I'm one too." There was a rapid exchange of glances. "Crack that, you poor boob!" they seemed to say.

Says Vanya, with perfect control: "What is your idea of a Lesbian, anyway? You say I'm a Lesbian. Why? Because you were reading my letters again? I know you, you sneak. I left the letters lying about purposely . . . yes, purposely. I want to put an end to this nonsense. I'm sick of this beating about the bush. Make up your mind one way or other. . . ."

Hildred intervened. "I'll settle this question myself," she said, turning on Tony Bring, her face scarlet. "I won't stand for this abuse any longer . . . do you hear that? If there's anything wrong in this house I'm the one who's responsible. Why don't you let up on her? Why don't you attack me, you coward? I can answer everything you want to know."

"All right then, *do it!*" he said.

Silence for a moment. A truck rolled by, shaking the building to its foundations.

"*Well* . . . what is it you want to know?" Hildred's foot is tapping impatiently.

"*Everything,*" he answered simply.

"Be specific. A minute ago you were making all sorts of

charges. Let's have them now, one by one . . . I'm ready for you."

A distressing weariness came over him. Suddenly it became too stupid for words. Like three balls on a billiard table. With the cue ball one took aim, and if the wrist worked in obedience to the laws of mechanics, ballistics, trigonometry, and whatnot, the red ball kissed the white ball and all three balls clicked. And if all three balls clicked that meant another shot. And if one could manage to keep all three balls bunched together, if one could nurse them along, as they say, one could have X over Y shots. He took a long shot and closed his eyes. He missed. It was somebody else's turn. He stood for a few moments looking on dumbly, dividing his attention between their silly, lying talk and his own restless fears.

Suddenly a remark of Hildred's reached him with telling effect. "What's that you're saying?" he shouted fiercely. "Stop it, do you hear? Another word and I'll crack you! By God, you people are capable of anything . . . *anything*. You stand there trying to tell me that you thought I might be . . . ? Listen, if you ever use that word in connection with me I'll brain you. You tell me you were jealous . . . jealous of a friend of mine. God damn it, if I thought you were telling me the truth I'd kick the guts out of you. But I don't believe you . . . I don't! You're a liar from the bottom up. You'd lie if they were putting the noose around your neck. You're lying now because you don't know how to crawl out of it. You'd say I was insane if you thought you could save your face. You'd say anything! You're corrupt, you're poisoned, you're diseased! So you thought I was a homo once . . . or almost one. That's rich . . . rich . . . rich. Jesus, I'm going to put on a red necktie and advertise myself. Maybe I could bring a little money in too if I were persevering. A homo to rent—by the week or month—moderate terms. A *respectable* homo, with a wife and family. . . ."

Throughout this scene, which became increasingly violent and coarse, Vanya sat rigid, her lips sealed, a look of stony impenetrability on her countenance. Now and then, when some particularly vile epithet was hurled in her direction, a shudder went through her. As for Tony Bring, he seemed to have lost his senses. Back and forth he strode, shaking his fist first at Hildred, then at Vanya. The most shocking, virulent obscenity poured from his lips. He cursed them up and down, denounced them in the foulest terms. Through it all Vanya had managed to preserve her Sphinx-like imperturbability. But when, in a final gust of passion, when dancing before her on tiptoes, threatening her, reviling her, spitting at her feet, he shouted "Louse!" she could tolerate no more. Springing to her feet, her eyes twitching like a maniac's, she returned insult for insult, curse for curse. It ended with hysterical convulsions of grief and rage. Hildred flung herself on the bed and tried to stifle her sobs in the pillow. Her sobs left Tony Bring cold. It's gone home at last, has it? he thought to himself. Good! Let her lie there and taste some of the agony of life.

After a lull he turned to Vanya, who had by now calmed down a bit, and said in his most conciliatory vein: "Now that the fireworks are over, let's talk things over sensibly. Let's see if we can't understand one another."

Vanya was pacing to and fro, her eyes still wild, her fingers working frantically. Thin streams of smoke spurted from her nostrils, her bosom was covered with ash. Keen as a blade, venomous, belligerent, she was on fire from tip to toe. What had just transpired was simply a workout for her. She was furious to think that Hildred had succumbed so wretchedly. It was cowardice, sheer, feminine cowardice, and it was disgusting. She was not only ready with her tongue, but with her hands. Let him only try . . . let him only put a little finger on her! She'd break him in half . . . splinter him . . . mangle him.

Asked if she felt like participating, Hildred made no answer; her shoulders shook convulsively, her head sunk a little deeper into the pillow. Clearly then it was between the two of them. And it was clear too that Vanya approved as, with lips grimly compressed and eyes wide and unseeing, she nodded for him to continue.

But from the moment he opened his lips and as if in accompaniment to his words, there began to pass through her head a strange procession of figures—grotesques in wood and ivory, with taut, elongated breasts, their strange limbs embellished by dyes of raw blue and red. One of them, a figure from the Sudan, sat on a tabouret upheld by a cluster of smaller figures. A thin, delicate column shot from the cavity of the thorax to the genitals. But its phenomenal aspect resided rather in an object which elevated itself from the plateau formed by the monster's lap. In the museum, where she had seen it recently, people scrutinized it minutely, shook their heads, held whispered, animated conversations to one side, their gaze still riveted to the object clasped by the rigid, painted fingers. Bisexual it was—phallus and lingam combined, though to say this was to give nothing of its exotic character. To penetrate its significance one would be obliged to retrace the entire development of the race, to enter not only into the mystic ceremonials of primitive man, but to go back further still, back to the ferocious nuptial orgies of the insect world, world of sexual anomalies, world of lust and terror beyond all power of human conception.

Such were the thoughts that passed through her head as

she listened to his words. God knows, his thoughts too were anything but ordinary. They seemed to follow the course of his words like a river canalized by the shoulders of a gorge. The solid, resisting walls were choking the tumultuous stream that rose somewhere far back in the myriad roots of his soul; it was their function, doubtless, to stand thus unyielding, throttling the blind, destructive energism which would otherwise devastate the world and itself come to naught. His thoughts surging forward and upward swirled in vast eddies, rose in dazzling foam and spray to collapse again and be borne along in a lathery chute. The most that could be hoped for in this ceaseless struggle was a triumph of erosion. Thus, confusedly, the conflict shaped itself in his thought. His language was far less complicated. It was like the difference between sound and script in music. What the tongue expressed was but the thin melody which held the extravagant weave of thought and feeling together.

As he went on his voice became more soothing and gentle; he paused now and then, expecting that she would seize the occasion to inject a word, but she remained silent, her hostility falling away more and more. He reminded her briefly of a scene only a few days back when Hildred had locked herself in the little room. What went on in there behind the bolted door? Ah, what a question to ask. As if he could expect them ever to tell. But this much they had admitted—after frightful wrangling, after he had literally extorted it from them—*they went in there to kiss each other!* Well, no use running on in this vein. Perhaps the best solution was to submit the case to a jury—an impartial tribunal of experts. Let each one choose his man. Let each one tell his own story.

At this point Hildred suddenly came to life.

"You shut your bloody mouth!" he yelled.

"No, leave her be!" said Vanya. "She's in this just as much as we."

"She's out of it, and she's to keep her mouth shut, I say. Are you willing to agree to my suggestion?" he said, turning his back on Hildred.

It was like the critical moment in a fight, when one of the contestants suddenly softens under a damaging blow. He was for rushing her to her knees, but again Hildred intervened. "She will do no such thing," she said, rising from the bed with a sort of dying-empress dignity. It was a ridiculous proposal through and through. There *were* no experts competent to pass judgment. And besides . . .

"You mean to say . . ."

"I mean that no matter what anyone said it would make no difference to me."

"Even . . ."

"Even if the whole world agreed . . ."

"Agreed that what?"

"That she was queer . . . invert, pervert, whatever you like. No matter what they said I would never desert her. . . . Is that clear?"

It was quite enough. There comes a stage when the touch of reality becomes so sharp that one is no longer an individual harassed by circumstances, but a living being cut into slices. . . . That which a moment ago might have seemed like a living planet, a throb of splendor in a universe of night, becomes of a sudden a dead thing like the moon burning with fire of ice. In such moments all things are made clear— the meaning of dreams, the wisdom that precedes birth, the survival of faith, the stupidity of being a god, etc., etc.

Part 5

1

TONY BRING sat in the dark with his hands buried in his overcoat pockets, the collar turned up, his hat falling over his eyes. The place was cold and damp; it was like sitting in a tomb without even a taper burning. A fetid odor seeped from the walls—a sweet, sickening stench, full of leprosy. Thoughts gurgled through his brain like the music of the drains in Vanya's room. He thought about his thoughts as if they were smears under a lens.

The bell rang. Let it ring, he thought, I'm not here. There was a rap at the window, followed by a tattoo. He got up and pulled the curtain aside. His friend Dredge stood there grinning. He went through the lower hall and swung open the big gate. Dredge was still grinning.

"What are you doing with yourself in the dark?" asked Dredge.

"I was thinking, that's all."

"Thinking?"

"Yeah, don't you think sometimes?"

"Do you have to sit in the dark to think?"

He lit a candle while Dredge deposited himself in the most comfortable-looking seat and smiled his usual weak, affable

117

smile. It was Dredge's twenty-eighth birthday and he had had a drink or two in his room before stopping by. "You know," he said, "people go crazy from sitting around in the dark like this. I'll tell you what, you come over to my joint and have a little snifter with me. Then we'll go out and celebrate."

A LITTLE later they were sitting in Paulino's in the Village. The place was upside down. Everybody scrooched. A swell fraternity: gamblers, plainclothesmen, thugs, federal agents, big stews from the big papers, vaudeville teams, wisecracking Jews, faggots with dirty mouths, chorus girls, college boys with the signs of the zodiac stenciled on their slickers. . . . A free bottle of wine stood on every table. While they ate a crowd gathered in the hallway waiting to grab the vacated seats.

When they staggered out they had a beautiful edge on. As they walked down Sixth Avenue they were followed by an undersized pimp who insisted on handing them cards while he described more or less graphically the various women at his disposal. Next to a cigar store there was a dance hall. It was swamped. Booze again . . . vile, stinking booze. Where did it all come from? New York was just one big river of booze.

As they were leaning against the wall with ginger ale bottles in their hands suddenly they heard a scream and a hysterical young wench rushed out of the lavatory saying that she had been assaulted. A shot was fired, tables knocked over. In a jiffy, almost as if it were a Mack Sennett comedy, the cops appeared. They swarmed over the place, using their clubs liberally. They got hold of the young woman and bundled her out. And then the music started up and the waiters began mopping the floor. Nobody could say who had pulled the gun. Nobody seemed to want to know. Time to dance. Time to take another swig. Dredge looked around for a partner. All taken. It was like a bargain sale. They waited for the next dance. All taken. . . .

Outside the fellow with the cards was laying for them. He shook his head disparagingly. "Come with me," he urged. "Fifty nifty gals . . . and what I mean, they're nifty!"

"Tomorrow," said Dredge.

They ambled leisurely through the quaint old streets. The names of the dives were promising, but that was about all one could say for them. It was a bohemia without bohemians. The villainy, the vice, the joy, the misery—all was fictitious.

"I'm sick of the Village," said Dredge. He had been saying this for years.

Just then a door opened and they caught sight of a bar. They walked in without ceremony. It was one of those joints which are open to any and every one, from the President on down. Mahogany bar, brass footrails, soaped mirrors, calendars, photographs of pugilists and soubrettes clipped from the *Police Gazette*. The only innovation was the presence of the other sex. In the old days the female element kept to the back room. They weren't allowed to stand at the bar telling dirty stories or bragging about the number of men they had slept with. Nor did they need to be dragged out by a boat hook when the place closed. No, in the old days the women of the street sometimes conducted themselves like ladies, at least they tried to; the new age made it compulsive for the ladies to conduct themselves like whores.

At any rate, this was the conclusion the two of them came

to while indulging in a little quiet drinking. They discussed the situation backward and forward. They were annoyed that they should be obliged to rub shoulders with these respectable eighteen-year-old prostitutes.

They were walking toward Fifth Avenue, their way taking them through Washington Square, deserted now and silent. Near the arch they paused to void a little sentimentality. Once there was a charm to New York—the Haymarket, Huber's Museum, Tom Sharkey's, the German Village, and there was Barnum and Thomas Paine and O. Henry.... Gone all that. Skyscrapers now ... kikes, flappers, automats. Dredge opened up about the Luneta in Manila. A thousand times better off there, or in Nagasaki, where there were certain houses with red lights over the door and beautiful dolls with cherry-ripe lips and almond eyes....

A cab pulled up to the curb. The driver leaned out and beckoned to them. Would they like to know of a nice, quiet, refined place, etc.? To hear his dulcimer notes one would imagine that he had in mind a paradise of houris and musk.

Dredge was skeptical—it sounded too good, too much like the days when the Guadalquivir was ashimmer, etc.

"Hell," said the driver, "you don't want to go to some dive and get cracked over the bean, do you?" This by way of clinching the argument. "Get in," he purred, "and if you don't like it you can beat it. I wouldn't steer you to no gyp joint."

They no sooner got in than he started off hell-bent for election. "You'll like it all right," he shouted through the window.

The tone in which he flung this out irritated Dredge. "We don't have to like it," he shot back.

120

"Shut up!" said Tony Bring. "Don't start an argument with him. Let's see where he's taking us."

Somewhere in the 40s they rolled up in front of an imposing-looking office building. The entrance was barred by a folding gate. In the hallway stood a cop talking to the elevator boy. The five of them bundled into the elevator. As they ascended, the elevator boy whistled. He had a sallow, seamy face, the type one sees standing at the gallery entrance of burlesque theaters on a cold, rainy night.

There was a sprinkle of tinkling lights, carpets soft as velvet, doves glittering with sequins, their backs cool as alabaster, their vermilion lips trembling like wavelets. From a hidden alcove, subdued strains that made their limbs melt. An odor of sweetened bodies, heavy languor of roses, flurry of powdered limbs, goldfish dozing in tepid bowls. The door closed and the elevator dropped out of sight. They looked at each other helplessly. Trapped. Sorcerized. Locked in with the mystic bride.

There was someone at their elbow, pattering away in a suave, seductive tongue. Beside him stood the taxi driver, his hand outstretched. Tony Bring nudged his companion. "He wants you to slip him something."

"But I did," said Dredge.

"Well, give him some more then."

"For what?"

"For bringing us to such a nice, quiet, refined place."

THE GREEK who took them in tow proved to be a polite, smooth-faced assassin. He said yes to everything. His hands were pale and velvety and he had deep-set, roving eyes that glittered like agates. At the cloakroom they glanced around timidly. Gorgeous butterflies, dragging their cocoons, sailed by or paused to rest their wings, drugged by their own eroticism. In their passage they scattered a shower of petals and chatter thin as gauze.

The table to which they were conducted rose up like a drunken ship in a mist of smoking wine. Sparkle of silver and splintered crystal dissolving in fires of dust. Letters of pitch rising an inch thick from the menus. . . . The refinement of it made them shudder.

Hardly had they seated themselves when a pair of doves fluttered over. Dredge made an abortive effort to rise while Tony Bring rubbed his hand over his beard meditatively and glanced at his frazzled shirt in the mirror beside him. The introductions were brief and pleasant. The Greek rubbed his smooth, velvety hands. His tongue moved smoothly between his smooth white teeth. Everything smooth as a bright new scabbard.

Miss Lopez, of Spanish blood and somewhat oversexed, inquired at once if they weren't thirsty. She asked it in a parched voice, as if the past were a monsoon and her life a desert. The other, Miss St. Clair, expressed herself as just dying to dance. She got hold of Dredge and, in her refined way, dragged him to the floor for a workout. Miss Lopez employed a different strategy. She had the trick of appearing to swoon in one's arms.

They were scarcely seated when the orchestra struck up again, whereupon Miss Lopez became electrified. It was one of those specialty numbers which provide an opportunity for the singer to circulate from table to table and pour out her heart as the music bursts open the windows of her soul. Miss

Lopez paused just long enough at each table to touch the pocketbook of the one on whom she fastened her drowning eyes, then stuffing the money in her bosom she gave a gratuitous wriggle or two and moved on—all without interruption, while the musicians repeated the chorus of the song over and over. It was a song about love. . . . "I love you . . . I love you . . ." There seemed to be scarcely any other words to it. The performance was concluded in front of the clover club cocktails which Dredge had ordered. As she imparted to the worn words a last lingering shred of tenderness, she sank to her seat like an angel breathing her last.

By now the girls had become extraordinarily thirsty. They asked for Sauternes, and when they had taken a few sips they excused themselves and fluttered away.

"Better count your dough," said Tony Bring.

Dredge pulled out his wad. There was thirty-seven dollars.

"Is that all you've got?" said Tony Bring.

"Is that *all* ?" Dredge did his best to look amazed.

"Listen, Dredge, pull yourself together. This is a nice, refined place. . . ."

Dredge retreated behind his usual weak, amiable smile. "I don't know what's going to happen," he said, "and what's more I don't care. I've been thrown out of better places than this. Forget about it!"

But Tony Bring couldn't forget—not all at once, at any rate. He was thinking of the taxi driver's words . . . and then that smooth-faced assassin with the velvety paws!

When the girls returned they remarked immediately that the boys looked pensive. Miss Lopez leaned on Tony Bring's shoulder and whispered something in his ear. Her hand burned right through his trousers. "Just one little kiss," she whispered, and, lying back in his arms, she pulled his head down, fastened her warm lips to his mouth, and hung there. The lights grew dim and as the first muted notes of "The Kashmiri Song" throbbed in their ears she clung to him rapturously. All about them were panting nymphs expiring in the arms of their partners. It was like a warm night in spring below the Himalayas when the pigeons begin to rut, when among the wet leaves of the forest there begins a rustling and murmuring, a bursting of fragrant buds, an imperceptible movement and stir that thickens the blood.

"I adore that shirt you're wearing," Anita whispered, as she snuggled up close. She had dropped the Lopez after the second dance.

Tony Bring looked at himself again in the mirror. "It's the only shirt I've got," he stammered.

Hearing this, Miss St. Clair was in stitches. "His only shirt!" She repeated it several times, tossing her head back and holding her sides in order not to burst with laughter.

"It's the truth," he declared. "I haven't a red cent to my name."

Anita looked at him darkly and gave him a playful poke in the ribs. "I know," she said, rolling her eyes demurely. "I've heard that before."

Dredge was taking it all in with a big grin. It didn't matter much to him whether they were put out now or later. It was a good jest and nobody seemed depressed over it.

The young ladies seemed to have bladder trouble—they excused themselves again. They were scarcely gone this time when the waiter appeared. It was a new waiter, more formally attired than the previous one, more *hauteur* to his bearing. Without addressing a single word to them he presented the bill. Dredge looked at the bill and then at the waiter. "We're not going yet," he said, trying to look unconcerned.

Now it's coming, thought Tony Bring.

The waiter stood by stiffly while Dredge emptied his pockets. He slapped his withered-looking bills on the table. The waiter counted without seeming to touch them. Then, with a brusque, arrogant move, he seized the bill and shoved it under Dredge's nose. "Fifty-five dollars!" he said.

"For what?" said Dredge. "For what?"

"Listen, Dredge, don't argue about it!"

"But where the hell am I going to get fifty-five dollars? You know what I've got. That's what I'm giving him and that's all he's going to get." Saying which he picked up the money and shoved it in his pocket.

Presently the Greek was standing beside them, rubbing his paws. He had been taking it all in from a distance. "What seems to be the trouble?" he asked, his tone pleasant and conciliatory.

The waiter mumbled in his ear.

"Oh, that's it?" He appeared completely taken by surprise. He turned to Dredge, his voice still cordial, conciliatory, smooth, and affable. He put a few polite questions forward and then, as if the idea had just occurred to him, he remarked: "Perhaps you'd better come with me and talk this over with the credit manager. We ought to be able to straighten this little thing out satisfactorily. It's only a matter of fifty-five dollars."

Tony Bring sat tight and stared at the wall. He wondered how Dredge would handle "this little thing." The girls had not returned. The music was still playing, but it sounded less intoxicating now. The glasses had been removed, the table was bare.

Time dragged. Nobody came near him. He fidgeted about and rubbed his hands over his fuzzy beard. The button of his collar had come off.

Presently Miss St. Clair appeared. Anita had been requested to sit at another table for a while. Wouldn't he like to order her another cocktail? Just one? And where was his friend? All this with the most astonishing naiveté. Told that Dredge was trying to settle the bill, she put her hand over her mouth and yawned.

"Buy me just one little drink," she pleaded.

"But I can't! I haven't a cent on me."

"You mean that?" said Miss St. Clair. This time she seemed to sense the truth of his words. There was not only scorn in her voice, but fright, as if he had suddenly pulled a lizard out of his pocket and dropped it in front of her.

An awkward moment or two intervened. They sat there without looking at each other, she drumming furiously with her fingertips, he looking at a mural over her head which portrayed a Svengali clawing at a group of dipsomaniacs with long pointed nails.

When at last Dredge returned he was wreathed in smiles. He was escorted as before by the Greek, his factotum, and the regular waiter. "What'll you have to drink?" were his first words. "A little Scotch for me," he said to the waiter. And then, with a touch of irritation—"Where's Anita? Tell her we want her."

He sat down. "Everything's O.K." he said. "Go ahead and enjoy yourself. If you don't like Anita we'll get someone else. We're paying for service and we're going to get it."

"Listen, Dredge, this is amusing, but what's the dope? I'm sitting here on pins and needles."

Dredge extracted a cigar from his breast pocket, bit the end off leisurely, and between puffs proceeded to unbosom himself. "Simple," he said. "They wanted to know if I had a bank account and where and how much. I gave them Keith's bank. How can they tell? They made me wait until they investigated. *Investigate!* How the hell can they investigate at this hour of the night? Finally they said everything was jake and handed me a blank check to sign."

"Then everything's O.K.?"

"O.K. Have anything you like."

Anita returned with Miss St. Clair, sat down very sweetly, and bathed them in her warm, Andalusian blood. The night wore on. Champagne flowed, and Malaga—because Anita had succumbed to a fit of *Heimweh*. They spoke of bullfights which they had never seen, and Dredge tried to talk about interesting things like the Luneta in Manila and the chewing-gum mines in Mexico. Every so often a bouncer appeared and dragged some poor intoxicated devil to the rear where with the assistance of a cop and a taxi driver the third degree was administered.

It was dawn when Tony Bring said good-bye to Dredge. In the lower hall it was still dark. He tripped and fell against the door. The glass rattled. Then silence, a deep, mysterious silence. He pushed the door open and felt around in the dark for a candle.

"Is that you?" came Hildred's voice.

He stumbled over to the bed with the candle in his hand.

127

Someone was in the bed with Hildred, lying face downward, dead to the world.

"Who's that?" he demanded.

"My God, but you're drunk!" cried Hildred.

"Never mind. . . . Who's lying there? Is it Vanya?"

"Shhhhh!"

"Don't shush me! Get her up . . . quick! Who told her she could sleep in my place? Hey, wake up there! Hey, Vanya!"

Vanya turned over stupidly and blinked. He put the candle on the floor and, slipping his arms under her, started lugging her out of the bed.

"Hold on! Wait a minute!" she cried. "What *is* this, anyway?" Suddenly she got a whiff of his breath. *"Drunk again?"*

"Drunk nothing. Where do you come off sleeping in my bed?" And with this he pulled more violently.

"Let go of me . . . you're wrenching my arms out!" she screamed.

Hildred tried to drag him off. He swung out blindly and caught her in the pit of the stomach. She gave a groan and sank to the floor. In an instant Vanya was beside her. "Quick . . . get some water!" she cried. "She's hurt."

"Get it yourself! I didn't touch her. A nice how-do-you-do, coming home and having to fight your way into bed. This is *my* bed, understand? Keep out of it hereafter."

Vanya rushed to the bathroom. Hildred was lying on the floor where she had tumbled, pressing her hands against her groin and moaning. Tony Bring collapsed on the bed. "Why do you people have to make such a scene?" he groaned. "Can't a fellow have a little jag on once in a while without all this fuss? Come on, don't lie there like a sick mule. Shake a leg!"

He let out a tremendous lionlike roar and rolled over. "Jesus, everything's spinning. That champagne . . . that was too much. Too much." He began singing in a quavering falsetto. "Let me call you sweetheart, I'm in love with you-ou-ou . . ."

"Shut up!" said Vanya, shaking him roughly. "You'll wake the neighbors."

"Where's Hildred? Why don't she come to bed? I want this monkey business cut out . . . *understand?*"

Vanya spoke to him gently, undid his clothes, and pushed him under the blankets. Then she got a wet towel and wrapped it around his head. "That's fine," he said. "Vanya, you're a brick."

A little later Vanya had to help him to the bathroom; she held him up while he bent over the tub and vomited. "That's rotten," he said, as he leaned against her and smiled wryly. "You get out of here . . . I'll mop it up." But as he bent over his very bile seemed to rise to his throat and he grew deathly sick. "What a pig I am! What a pig!" He begged her to leave him alone, he would be all right in a little while. It was then he noticed that he was standing before her in his underwear. He looked at her and smiled weakly, like Dredge—that foolish, insipid grin. He saw himself in the mirror, his face green, his eyes puffed and inflamed, his mouth soiled.

"Where's Hildred?" he said. "Did I hurt her? What did I do? I didn't hit her, did I?"

Vanya had taken the towel from his head and was cleaning the tub with it. The odor was vile.

"Come," he said weakly, "don't bother about that, I'll take care of it in the morning. Get hold of me . . . I'm weak as a cat."

Back in bed Vanya removed his soiled garments and

wrapped him in the blankets. "That's it," she murmured, while he groaned and shivered. "That's it . . . go to sleep! Everything is fine, Tony. Don't worry. There . . . there . . ." And she padded the blankets about him snugly.

He passed out immediately. Meanwhile Vanya slipped back to her room and squeezed into the narrow cot with Hildred. "It was nothing," she murmured, as she put her arms about Hildred. "He just got sick and puked up."

Soon they too were sleeping peacefully. All was silent as a crypt—except in the street, where every now and then someone passed and gave a nervous, meaningless little cough.

2

———————⬩———————

A THIN coat of snow had fallen during the night. All over Christendom on this bright, frosty morning people were saying "Merry Christmas!" to one another and then going to church to shed a few tears. Not even the most hardened atheist could escape the infectious spirit of Christmas. For weeks the Salvation Army had kept its beggars posted at vantage points throughout the city; the men, looking like debauched monks, stood beside a huge caldron heaped with money and rang a little dinner bell; the women, too, rang their bells and held out tambourines with their thin, frozen fingers. The purpose of all this was to bring peace on earth, to keep the derelicts of the great metropolis from going astray, from drinking themselves to death, or joining the Communist Party. Everybody knew what a blessing the Salvation Army was and what godly work the rescue missions were doing down in the slums, in Chinatown, along the Bowery— everywhere that poverty, vice, and evil flourished. And everyone, as he passed these emaciated Kris Kringles, these dolorous sisters of mercy who sang so beautifully when the bass drum sounded, threw in a few coppers and felt that he had done something to help the good cause along.

131

The department stores spoke of *good* Christmases and *bad* Christmases. In some vague, super-arithmetical way the profits were supposed to redound eventually to the Savior's glory. All during the busy weeks that preceded the day, people spoke in terms of shirts, stickpins, books, cameras, etc. It was only at the eleventh hour, during that brief intermission when the choir wreaked its grief and anguish, that the Savior Himself was thought of. What a spectacle it was for Him up there in the clouds, sitting on the right-hand side of God the Father, listening to the bells pealing, seeing all those poor bums on the Bowery standing in line waiting for the big handout. And how precious were His feelings when He looked down over the dark places of the world, into the heathen lands, and saw there men who were not Caucasians—yellow men, black men, men with kinky hair, men with rings in their noses and breasts tattooed—saw all of them raising their eyes heavenward to bless His name, to sing their hallelujahs.

Tony Bring was awake somewhat earlier than usual this bright, frosty morning. He was awakened by a terrific, unslakable thirst. They were all thirsty, as a matter of fact, only the effort of getting out of bed and going to the sink was too painful for the others. He reminded Hildred that it was time to get up, that it was growing late, but Hildred lay there like a log, gently pressing a wet towel against her eyelids.

"Damn it," he said, "we're not going to disappoint them today. I won't do it!"

While Hildred feebly bestirred herself he took a seat beside the window and began browsing through the volumes of Proust which she had given him as a Christmas gift. On the gut table was an enormous bouquet of gardenias—Hildred's gift to Vanya. The earthy, sensuous odor, combined with the insane procession that moved in a St. Vitus' dance on the walls, produced in him an exquisite mélange of emotions, intensified by the sight of Hildred lying there in the dim light, her face white as a death mask, her lips parting now and then to emit a feverish groan. He fell to thinking about the man who had given to the world these inexhaustible volumes, the sick little giant chained to his bed who, with a dying strength, had written his precious entomology of society in a room hermetically sealed, his body wrapped in clothes and blankets, the table covered with notebooks, with medicines and drugs and opiates. Here was a man whose life had been filled with suffering, and by his supreme art he had converted it into music sublime and unforgettable.

Parallel with these speculations there developed in his mind another train of thought—the realization that in a little while he would be standing before his aged parents, meeting their questioning eyes, endeavoring by a futile chaffering to drive from their minds the harassing awareness of his wasted years. It was this which made every Christmas a time of bitterness and regret, of melancholy and remorse. Each year that they gathered around the creaking table a sort of silent reckoning went on, a review of the past, of its follies and emptiness, of its griefs and disappointments. It was inevitable that sometime during the course of this solemn day mention should be made of the past, of the promise he had once shown, of the hopes they had placed in him, and so on. It was as if somewhere in that past—*when* he could no longer remember—there had been a line drawn, a division that placed hope on the far side, beyond the Alps, and despair on the near side, in the gray, desolate valley of the future. And

133

yet there was mingled with this atmosphere of gloom a tender sort of forgiveness, inexplicit, reserved, a melancholy
sympathy such as is lavished on the insane or the blind.

The volume which he held in his hands grew heavy. His
eyes, reverting to the text, saw there these curious words:
"We are attracted by every life that offers us something unknown, by a last illusion to be destroyed. . . ." It was at this
moment that Vanya came out of her room, clad in nightgown
and knee boots. "To be destroyed . . . to be destroyed . . ."
The words repeated themselves, like a refrain—better still,
like a note held by an invisible singer when some minute
obstacle in the path of the needle prevents it from moving
along its destined course. As she stood before him, a be-
draggled, hoydenish slut, the phonograph in his brain kept
singing—"to be destroyed . . . to be destroyed . . ." En-
chanted by the thought of what a queer effect would be
produced were he then and there to explode this ringing
note, he suddenly burst out laughing—a tremendous, uncontrollable roar that brought Hildred to her feet.

"That's a hell of a way to get me out of bed!" she yelled.

"Merry Christmas!" he yelled. "And get the cowbells out!"

"He's still drunk," said Vanya, affecting an air of disgust.

"Listen, old hook and ladder, I'm not drunk . . . and by the
way, thanks for the shirt . . . it's swell, only it's not my size."

While they toddled off to the bathroom he got busy, lit a
candle, and began to inspect the mattress. What a night it had
been! Gardenias and Chartreuse, Marcel Proust and the odor
of fumigation . . . and Dredge dropping in to wish them "a
Merry Christmas," but remaining until four A.M. to talk about
lice and the microcosmic hosts in the petroleum beds. He
turned from the mattress to the gut table. It was strewn with
cigarettes, empty bottles, broken chess pieces, sandwiches,

gardenias, *Sodom and Gomorrah*, mistletoe, caricatures by the Bruga woman, the *Firebird* in smithereens. In the armchair were the gifts Hildred had received from her admirers: silk hose, brassieres, perfume, shawls, cigarettes, books, candy, bottles of liqueur (all empty), manicure sets, cold cream jars, black step-ins . . . enough to fill a few pages of Sears Roebuck's catalogue. He sorted out a few objects with the intention of presenting them to the family. His mother always admired the stockings Hildred wore; it didn't matter if the size was a little off—they were expensive, that was the principal thing. For the old man he laid aside a carton of Camels, for his sister a manicure set which she would probably never use but which she would be thankful for just the same. For these trifles lifted from the swag he would be sure to receive the most effusive thanks from the old folks. His mother would be sure to murmur that they had been extravagant.

It was noon when the three of them marched down the stoop, their arms loaded with bundles. Hildred was dressed a little more conventionally than usual, but Vanya was in her usual rig—bare knees, black shirt, hair flung loose, etc. As they sailed out the bells commenced pealing. A little way down the street, in front of an ugly Lutheran church which had been given a fresh coat of mustard for the holidays, a knot of worshipers was breaking up and hastening away to heavy Lutheran repasts. Their eyes blazed as they caught sight of the incongruous trio standing on the corner, involved in a heated dispute.

A dispute on Christmas morning? Just so. All because Hildred felt bad about seeing Vanya go off alone.

"But supposing she changes her clothes?" Hildred was saying.

"It's too late. We'll have to take a cab as it is."

"Then I'm not going," and with this Hildred dropped her bundles in the street.

"Damn you!" shouted Tony Bring. "You're not going to leave me in the lurch now. What am I going to tell them?" Vanya begged them to wait just a few minutes—she would go inside and change quickly.

It was almost a half hour later when the two of them reappeared.

"Well, how do I look?" said Vanya.

"Fierce! Simply fierce! Where in Christ's name did you get that hat?"

"Well, you wanted me to look respectable, didn't you?" They hailed a cab. When they were within a block of their destination they stopped the cab and got out.

"Listen, Hildred, get her looking like something, will you?" he begged.

Hildred giggled. They were standing in front of a funeral parlor.

"This is no joke, Hildred. Christ, she looks like Bert Savoy."

They stood in front of the show window in which there was a beautiful satin-lined casket and worked over Vanya. But it was no use. "Give me that hat," he said, and when Vanya meekly surrendered it to him he crumpled it up and threw it in the gutter. "That's that!" he said. "Now come on . . . and look sad."

HIS MOTHER answered the doorbell. The smile which she had ready for them faded the instant she glimpsed Vanya. The old gent was cordial, though the glance he gave his son was enough to say, "Was it necessary to pull this off today?"

Hildred, in her characteristically frantic manner, began telling the folks immediately what a genius her friend Vanya was, how wealthy her parents were, how famously they got along together, and more twaddle that made Tony Bring shudder inwardly. He tried desperately to catch her eye, but she rattled on like an infant, absolutely indifferent, or else oblivious, to the impression she was making. There was a tense moment or two when Tony Bring's sister was introduced. No one knew exactly what was wrong with Babette. She was only a few years younger than her brother, but she had the mentality of a child of eight. She suffered besides from a strange nervous affliction: her limbs moved uncontrollably, her head would jerk from side to side as she talked and then droop down on her bosom. She had a way of prattling on interminably, switching rapidly from one subject to another without the least continuity, and she would go on like that until she was ordered to stop. No sooner was she introduced to Vanya, for instance, than she began to stuff the latter with a meticulous drivel about the affairs of the church; she related with marvelous facility and swiftness how wonderfully the choir had sung that morning and what the minister had said about the spirit of Christmas—how we should all love one another, not only on this day, but every day in the year. Suddenly she turned to her brother and, fixing him with a half-silly, half-reproachful smile, she exclaimed: "You should have been here this morning, Tony. I was thinking of you all the time. When did you get to bed last night? Did you buy a tree? He's a lovely man, our pastor. . . ."

"That's enough!" said the old gent, and Babette ceased instantly, though her head continued to roll loosely and then suddenly sank forward and rested on her bosom.

During the course of the meal it grew dark and they were obliged to light the tree. An eerie, sanctimonious glow flooded the table. Vanya and Hildred enjoyed the food enormously, expressing a regret however that there was not some good Rhine wine to wash it down. After the third course Hildred broke the ice by lighting a cigarette; Vanya, to the astonishment of all, fished out a bag of Bull Durham and rolled her own. Here Babette was moved to remark that *ladies* never smoked—at any rate, *she* never smoked, whereupon everyone, including her mother, burst out laughing. This spontaneous outburst precipitated an animated discussion. They detailed the latest marriages and births in the family, described the lovely funerals they had been to, reviewed the drink question, quoted the price of turkeys, spoke of the responsibilities weighing upon the President's shoulders and the speeches they had listened to over the radio; remarked that the Prince of Wales was a poor orator, likewise General Pershing. Babette got in a word or two now and then apropos the good work the church was doing. The old gent dwelt on the sad condition of business throughout the country. Finally they wanted to know what sort of pictures Vanya painted, whether she painted landscapes—because Mother didn't like the cows and sheep they had hanging in the parlor upstairs. It was explained that the old gent had bought them off a bartender one day, when he was in his cups, and he had paid a good price for them. Mother had an idea that Vanya's things might be more pleasant.

Hildred commenced to titter.

"I'll tell you, Mother," said Tony Bring, trying to hide his embarrassment, "I'm afraid you wouldn't care much for Vanya's paintings."

"Why, aren't they nice?"

"Oh, they're nice, sure . . . they're fine, but they're not the sort of pictures that would appeal to you."

The old man broke in. He understood quite well what Tony had in mind. Vanya was probably a *modern*. He turned to his wife—"You know those crazy things we saw in Loeser's last year . . . that's what she does most likely. Isn't that so, Tony?"

The latter looked at Vanya, who very charmingly took it into her head to toss a nod of acquiescence. The old man was quite pleased with his critical discernment.

"No rhyme nor reason to it . . . isn't that it?" he added.

"That's it, Father," Hildred chirped up. "They're all a little cracked. My friend Vanya, she's cracked too. . . ." She couldn't say any more because the idea had struck her as so amusing that she was growing hysterical. Tony Bring meanwhile was cursing her under his breath. It was such a good joke that everyone grew embarrassed over it. He was extremely relieved when Vanya, who by some miracle had attained to an amazing sense of discretion, switched the conversation to another topic. Life in the far West! Ah, how glorious it was! A gallop to the lake every morning, at dawn, a plunge into the icy waters, a meal outdoors over a wood fire. . . . (Nothing about the cult of the nude, thank God!) Satisfied with the effect she was producing, Vanya rambled on. She told them of her wanderings through Mexico and Central America, described for them in a language slightly mystifying the art and the customs of these far-off places.

"But weren't you afraid to travel about like that, all alone?" It was Tony Bring's mother who asked this.

His father spoke up instantly. "What?" he exclaimed. "*She* afraid? Why, she's just like a man, can't you see that?" He beamed at Vanya indulgently, as if he had just paid her a mark of the highest esteem. Hildred was on the point of breaking out again, but Vanya forestalled her.

And then Tony Bring spoke up too. "Yes, Mother," he said, "it was a fine, healthy life she lived out there. You can see what a wonderful constitution she has." Whereupon Vanya was subjected to a general scrutiny, quite like a picture which has escaped everybody's attention until suddenly some enterprising person points out its merits.

At this point Tony Bring's mother asked an embarrassing question. She wanted to know what they were doing to earn a living, and particularly whether Tony was doing anything. Hildred at once became serious. Tony had his book to finish, and after that—well, after that, she felt that they would be through with their worries.

"I think you're all a little daffy," said Tony Bring's mother. "I've been hearing about this book business for the last three years. How do you know he will get any money for it? There are so many writers already, and most of them are starving. I think he ought to look for a job. It's a disgrace to be slaving for him all the time. Why, you'll be an old woman before he's recognized."

"That's enough of that," said the old gent. "Mother always sees the gloomy side of things. Let's talk about something more cheerful. . . . How did you enjoy Christmas Eve? Did you go to the theater?"

Vanya and Hildred looked sheepish. It was left to Tony Bring to explain the wonderful time they had had.

Babette wanted to know if they had bought a tree. And how much did they pay for it? "We paid a dollar and a quarter for ours," she said. She told them where they could buy trimmings for the tree next year—very cheap.

Hildred invented a long yarn about the tree which they had

not bought. The folks listened with an absorbed air. Far more interesting, this yarn about the Christmas tree, than the tales which Vanya had spun about Mexico and Central America where the idols were hidden in the depths of the forests, and where the *chicleros* roamed with their machetes, gathering gum for the Wrigley Chewing Gum Corporation.

Toward evening they rose from the table, and while Babette helped her mother wash the dishes, Tony Bring seated himself in a rocker and gave ear to the old gent. The latter had grown pensive; he nestled back in his morris chair, his head propped up on one elbow, and mused aloud on the sad state of affairs in the financial world. He had lost the old animation which had endeared him to his barroom companions. It was fifteen years now since he had sworn off; whenever he referred to this turning point in his life it was with a note of mournful resignation, as if he had made a great blunder, for ever since that memorable day things had simply gone to the devil with him. One by one his customers were dying off, and no new ones appearing to take their places. The small fry, such as himself, were gradually being ousted by the big fellows, who in turn were forming still larger combinations. Everyone seemed to be hard up; some of his customers hadn't bought anything for the last five years. It were far better, said the old man, if people were to acquire the habit of spending money instead of saving it. It was one of those *bad* Christmases again.

As Tony Bring listened, it appeared to him that the old man was lapsing into senility. The old fire and sparkle was gone; he was just a shell filled with a hollow, plaintive murmur. Subdued and placid, the old man lay back in his armchair, baffled and paralyzed by the devastating march of events. He bemoaned the passing of the good old days, the passing of a generation whose customs and virtues he understood and respected. Once, for a brief spell, he had turned to religion, but the church, with its empty promises and its sad faces, proved even less hopeful than the Republican Party.

In the midst of these dreary speculations Hildred and Vanya had fallen asleep on the couch. Drugged by the meal, which they had devoured gluttonously, they rolled up like two cats and fell into a deep slumber. Tony Bring apologized for them by saying that they had been working very hard of late.

After a time his mother reappeared. She drew up a rocker, and folding her hands peacefully over her stomach, prepared herself for the enjoyment of a quiet little nap. But before dozing off she could not refrain from passing a few remarks. "You're not leading the right sort of life," she said. "It isn't fair to let Hildred work like that. You ought to be making something of yourself now." He had to listen all over again while she told him how futile it was to expect anything from his writing. *Scribbling*, she called it. "You were doing so well once. . . . Now you're leading a loafer's life, you drift from one thing to another, you have no money, nothing . . . nothing. You're going to regret it someday. And when we're gone what's going to become of Babette? Don't you ever think of her? Don't you ever think about the future?"

"Of course I do, Mother," Tony Bring answered. "But . . ."

"*But!* That's just it . . . always *but!*"

"But Mother, listen to me. . . ."

She put her hand up wearily. It was useless to try to deceive her. He might deceive himself, if he chose, but she was too old to be taken in by this nonsense of his. Babette listened to her mother with grave, round eyes that tortured him. Poor Babette, he thought, what will I ever do with her?

Meanwhile his father had dropped off to sleep. The bald head hung loosely from its bony hinge, the mouth had fallen open and remained thus, with that peculiar rigidity as of death. A few gray hairs which had formed a fringe above the large ears stuck out in thin wisps. Like a mummy, said Tony Bring to himself. Just like a mummy, with real hair and skin drawn tautly over the bones. . . .

The bell rang. It was a neighbor calling to see what a fine tree they had. Every now and then, in the course of a decidedly erratic conversation, he introduced the subject of Cain and Abel. But no one evinced the least concern in Cain and Abel. They would deliberately veer the conversation around to the Christmas tree, and put the glittering ornaments in his hand. He stayed but a few minutes, and then, so it seemed to Tony Bring, they deliberately ushered him out. In the vestibule, as he was being pushed toward the door, he stopped a minute and said good-bye again to Tony Bring. He wished him a very merry Christmas—and then, as if he were casually asking for directions to the subway, he inquired if the latter had any idea where the land of Nod might be.

"My son doesn't read the Bible," said Tony Bring's mother, and taking the man's hand, she shook it vigorously and opened the gate. When he was gone she explained that the poor man had lost his wife and child recently.

"He's religious," said Babette.

WHETHER IT was the result of the nap or the consoling reflection that he had narrowly escaped such a sad fate himself, at any rate, the old man suddenly came to and began to display some of his old verve. Bringing out a Berlitz primer, he explained to his son that he was studying French. It was a very handy thing to know, as he put it. He could say, in French, "How do you do," "How are things going with you," or "Take me to the Gare St. Lazare, I'm in a hurry." They were useful little expressions to have up one's sleeve in case one should ever go to France. What puzzled him were words like *fut*. He could never decide whether to pronounce it *foot* or *fee*.

"I wouldn't let those things disturb me, Father," said Tony Bring. "You'll probably never get to France anyway."

Hildred and Vanya had to be awakened for supper. They behaved just as if they were at home—grumbled, rubbed their eyes sleepily, yawned, clamored immediately for cigarettes, and then, playful-like, took to tickling each other. Finally they took it into their heads to wrestle, which the old man thought rather amusing. "Just like a man, isn't she?" he said. At this moment the two of them rolled onto the floor, their skirts up to their necks, their breasts spilling out. Coincident with this there was a loud snap and Babette came running in to see what had happened. Vanya and Hildred were sitting on the floor, adjusting their clothes, when Tony Bring's mother walked in.

"Mother, they broke the couch!" Babette exclaimed.

All eyes were turned on the couch; it was as still and solemn in the room as if someone had just expired there on the couch.

"Well, that's how you people take care of things," said Tony Bring's mother. "It lasted us twenty-five years."

Tony Bring was looking down at the floor. He waited a moment to hear what would follow. But there was nothing more. His mother had turned away and walked back to the kitchen. Her shoulders drooped a little more, so he thought.

But Hildred quickly got to her feet and followed his mother inside. "I'm dreadfully sorry," she said. "Please believe me. Have it fixed . . . tomorrow . . . I'll pay you for it."

The suggestion inspired no emotion.

"You have quite enough to pay for," said Tony Bring's mother in a resigned voice. "No, don't feel badly about it. It's time we had a new one anyway."

"But Mother, you like this couch . . . I know how it is. I had no idea such a thing would happen."

"No, of course you didn't. You see, we're not so wild as you young people. We're getting more subdued now. . . ."

Tony Bring was standing by. "Listen, Mother, don't throw it out. Do as Hildred says. It's much better than getting a new couch." And while he offered profuse apologies he took Hildred by the arm and squeezed it viciously. Soon afterward they sat down to supper and once again the tree was lighted and the table flooded with a weird, sanctimonious glow.

Thus they got through the day.

As they left the house Babette shouted after them to say that she would be down soon to have a look at Vanya's pictures. Turning back for a last farewell, Tony Bring saw the old folks standing at the railing looking up at the sky. Guess it'll rain tomorrow, he said to himself.

When they had passed the funeral parlor Hildred whistled for a cab. Not a word passed between them until they were almost home. Then suddenly Hildred announced her intention of going on to the Village to buy some wine.

"I'll go along," he said.

No, she didn't want that. She would return immediately. They were still arguing about the matter when the cab drew up to the door.

"You promise to be back in an hour?"

"In less than that," she said.

IT WAS almost dawn when they came staggering down the street singing "Onward Christian Soldiers." Once inside they collapsed. Vanya lay on the floor with an empty bottle in one hand and a chocolate layer cake in the other. Hildred had to be laid out like a corpse and undressed. In her drunken lingo she muttered foul accusations against some devil who had drugged their drinks. "Merry Christmas, Tony! Merry Christmas!" she cried. Then she took to mewing like a cat, after which she became repentant and murmured: "I'm sorry I broke the couch, honest I am. You don't love me anymore, do you? I'm not drunk, dear, I'm ill. . . . Some dirty bastard drugged us. . . ."

Vanya he allowed to remain on the floor, stepping over her as if she were a mangy dog. They clamored for wet towels and ice. Hildred wanted paregoric. Vanya wanted doughnuts and coffee.

"Wouldn't you like some nice mountain oysters?" he jeered.

"Please light the fire," Hildred moaned in a low agonizing voice. "I'm ill. . . . I'm not drunk, I tell you."

"*Allez à la Gare St. Lazare . . . je suis très pressé.*"

"I'm freezing. . . . Please light the fire!"

"You poor kid, you want me to make you a nice little fire?"

"Please, Tony, please. . . ."

"I'll make you warm," he said. "Just wait a minute." And he went to his file case, emptied the contents on the hearth, and put a match to it. As the blaze leaped up a weird glow suffused the room; the walls quivered and the figures began to dance.

"Feel better?" he asked, and he put his foot through the file case and splintered it. "You didn't think I'd let you freeze to death, did you?" He took the chairs one by one and smashed them also.

"That's it!" cried Hildred. "Burn them up . . . burn everything . . . tomorrow we'll get new furniture."

There was a crackle and roar as the flames shot up the flue. "That's wonderful . . . *wonder*ful," groaned Hildred. "You're so good, Tony. I want you to have a merry, merry Christmas."

"Merry Christmas!" yelled Vanya. "Don't you *love* it?"

"You poor little bums," he said. "So they tried to poison you, did they? The idea!"

He sat on the gut table and watched the flames licking up ten years of scribbling. Where was the land of Nod? The land of Nod was in the noodle and Cain and Abel were a couple of gaudy fellows with red neckties. *Comment allez-vous? Très bien, monsieur, et vous-même?* Imagine it—someone trying to drug two little ladies on Christmas day! Where in Christ's name did she get that hat? A swell casket, it was—satin-lined. Just like a man . . . so healthy. And in the depths of the forests were monstrous idols, their eyes glowing with gems . . . a wilderness through which the *chicleros* roamed searching for chewing gum. Slot machines for clean white teeth. Drive me to the Gare St. Lazare, I'm in a hurry. . . .

3

———————◆———————

NEW YEAR'S EVE! America trying to stand on its hind legs.
Every one wall-eyed, scrooched, crocked. Dredge fried to the
hat and Hildred down with the screaming meemies. A great
jamboree in which Vanya delivers herself of a jolly little poem
about the virgin spittle of the gutter, the seven cathedrals that
gave warm milk, and the dead rats floating in the Seine. Bob
Ramsay drops in with his friend Homer Reed and Amy,
Homer Reed's mistress, the three of them followed by a slutty
little bitch which insists on leaving its card here and there.
Wrestling bouts between Amy and Vanya, between Vanya
and Hildred, between Hildred and Amy. The referee getting
down on his haunches to see that there are no foul tactics and
what kind of underwear, if any, there may be. Amy fighting
like a wildcat, her clothes ripped to shreds, her face puffed
and gory. And then Emil Sluter pops in and a Jew named
Bunchek. Anecdotes concerning a female called Iliad who
has a crush on her own mother. A droll affair this—jealousy,
intrigue, incest. Sluter, the polite bastard with the butter-
colored gloves, listening with both ears cocked. "And who
was the mother jealous of, if I'm not indiscreet?" Hildred, in
her incandescent state, blurting out—"Why, of me!"

"Of you? No! Well, I'll be go to hell. . . . Did you hear that, Tony?"

Tony Bring hears only too well. He is thinking of the oily phrases Sluter will palm off on him next time they meet. "Golly, man, I tell you, one has no idea with what a terrific force these things can sweep down on you and destroy you; and it's all the more insidious because it finds you unprepared. Hasn't that been your experience?" That is Sluter's lingo: full of modifying clauses, prefatory notes, retractions, apologies, innuendoes, discreet loopholes, fire escapes. . . .

Meanwhile there's Hildred emptying her mind like a slop pail. And Bunchek, the pimply-faced gawk, gaping goggle-eyed. Hildred, the wife, sitting with her legs parted, her stockings rolled down, her thighs showing, her legs bruised and scratched. Informing all and sundry about her strong spine and the little hollow just above the tip of the spine which everyone admires so when they dance with her. Still not enough about it—elaborating, embroidering, begging Homer Reed to put his hand there—because, as an artist, he can appreciate these accidentals, these anatomical nuances.

Then Bunchek, pianissimo at first, opening up with a tender minuet from the *Kama Sutra*, followed in brief order by the fully orchestrated works of Stekel, Jung, and Pavlov. Not a mind, but a cesspool. Much too much, even for Hildred's strong stomach. Sluter, always correct, excusing himself in order to go outside and stick his finger down his throat.

And finally, Amy, spurred on by her consort, stripping down to her pantalettes and giving a slow muscle dance. Not finally, either, because immediately following this Bunchek and Ramsay commence a word-reaction contest: luck-duck, brick-pick, runt-bunt, mass-crass, ore-core, flit-sit.

Sluter joins in, and then Hildred; the room is filled with the sound of words coupling and uncoupling: dingo-bingo, righto-presto, bigboy-frigeroi, Lucy-juicy, tart-cart, spiddivus-quiddibus, Apennine-turpentine, souse-louse. . . . Until station D-R-E-D-G-E announces the birth of the homunculus with Father Aquinas patching the shingles of his roof to keep the angels out. A little spiel about the gastronomic functioning of the unicellular organism and then: "The Alps and the Andes are but so much hardened ocean ash, and perhaps the whole earth is but the compact mold of dead things." A fine coprolalic orgy watered with sexual proverbs and neologisms like *dingitaries* and *vaginaries*. Sluter remaining after the others have gone to take a stirrup cup. Avid to sponge up a few fundamental verities, as, for example—

1. "How did the world then come to be filled with life?"
2. "Just what is meant by the Symbolist Movement?"
3. "Am I right in saying that Gauguin was perhaps a little too decorative?"

Ushering in the dawn with *Spiddividdibeebumbum*. . . .

THE NEW Year! New resolutions, new quarrels, new ideas afoot. Paris again. And from Vanya a leitmotif: Sweden. Sweden! And why Sweden? Sweden: land of the midnight sun, of fjords and staggering hors d'oeuvres, land of liberty for the third sex, the star-spangled bananas for Lesbians and Uranians.

Intermission while Vanya and Hildred toy with the idea of finding more suitable employment. Whims. Caprices. Hallucinations.

During the intermission someone puts the bug into their heads to see Paul Jukes. Paul Jukes: the greatest painter alive! Doesn't think much of Cézanne, and less of Matisse. As for Picasso—the only thing, according to Paul Jukes, that Picasso ever mastered is the art of drawing mechanical ducks. None of your mechanical ducks and linoleum patterns for Paul Jukes. Not on your tintype! The greatest American painter that ever lived is a stickler for muscles and green fields, for doing the right breast as religiously as the left, for putting heads on torsos and not lilac bushes or cauliflowers. If you want to draw a man, you must first have arms and legs. . . . *Alors*, see Paul Jukes. Perhaps Paul Jukes can use a model or two. He who can tie a brush to his behind and paint the aurora borealis, perhaps such a much can give a word or two of advice—or a ticket for Sweden. Nothing definite in mind. See Paul Jukes, that's all. . . .

Iⴀ so happened that the day chosen for the interview was one of those *bad* days. The great Paul Jukes, only released from the hospital a few days previously, was getting ready to bring suit against his physician for puncturing his bladder. He was feeble and crotchety. He didn't even have the courtesy to invite his unknown guests inside.

They went away crestfallen. The great Paul Jukes—bah! Vanya spat on the sidewalk to void her disgust. Phew! Pfui! As for Hildred—Hildred wasn't satisfied to merely spit on the sidewalk. She had to do something extra. She called him "a horse's ass."

A day or so afterward they had another idea. Hildred's idea this time. "Models wanted for hosiery and lingerie . . . easy work . . . only a few hours a day." Why not grab off a little easy money? Why not?

Bright and early they rose one morning. Even Tony Bring

was required to lend a hand. He took a big brush, with a long, curved handle, and curried Vanya's back. They took the knots out of her hair, laundered her bloomers, and pressed her blue cheviot suit. As a finishing touch Hildred sprinkled toilet water over Vanya's shirtwaist. All set. Vanya gay as a sparrow straddling a telegraph wire. Wiggling her behind a little, à la Margie Pennetti. Ravishing. What has she been concealing all this time? Too utterly utter. . . .

But when they returned Hildred had a long face. Some dirty little kike with a tape measure had gotten fresh—with Vanya particularly. He had gone over them as if they were race-horses. And there was no screen. They had to undress in the presence of three dirty little kikes. The one held the tape measure, the other put the measurements down on a pad, and the third—the third, it seems, just stood by like a life buoy to see that nothing went wrong. He was working away all the while on a big Havana cigar. The climax came when it was discovered that Vanya had to be measured for the third time. It was all due to an error on the part of the gentleman with the pencil and pad. He didn't have his mind on his business, apparently. Imagine, he had nothing to do but get the numbers right—but when they looked at the numbers, the numbers were phony. To aggravate matters, Vanya, it seems, had taken it all as a big joke. Even when they were fooling around her crotch she displayed the same disgusting *sang-froid*. She wasn't even concerned enough to hold her hands over her bosom.

"No moral sense whatever" was Hildred's angry comment.

"But what did I do?" Vanya cried. "Didn't you get undressed too? Do you think you looked more respectable because you kept your damned brassiere on?"

"That isn't it! It's the way you stood there."

"What did you expect me to do—stand there like *September Morn*? Jesus, what a prune you can be!"

THINGS WERE going swell during the intermission, except that Hildred was getting in dutch at the Caravan. They were threatening to fire her if she didn't mend her ways.

"You'd better nurse the job," cautioned Tony Bring. "Things'll be going to hell around here otherwise."

Vanya agreed. Someone had to show a sense of responsibility.

But there was another, a more important reason, why Hildred ought to carry on. Vanya had taken to fiddling around again with plaster and whatnot. She was threatening to make more Count Brugas, more masks and casts. Money was needed. Of course, once Hildred had sold a few everything would go swimmingly. And where was there a better market than the Caravan? Lausberg would probably start the ball rolling; and then there was that big, good-natured slob Earl Biggers, to say nothing of Iliad's mother and the boys with the golden locks who just loved anything artistic.

Hildred was not the sort to nibble at a line. She gobbled it up, hook, bait, and sinker. There was genius in the idea. Naturally! A genius had conceived it. A Romanoff genius.

Now she came home from work immediately. Everyone chipped in. If a visitor arrived, he was given a hammer and saw, or else they instructed him how to tear sheets of brown wrapping paper into thin strips. The floor was a morass: plaster of Paris, sawdust, nails, varnish, glue, pieces of velvet and satin, dolls' wigs, Mexican dyes . . . the disorder of a burlesque show backstage.

For practice they made casts of each other. Hildred refusing to put up with the ordinary, placid, deathlike composure. Always striving for the grotesque. Instead of likenesses, therefore, they turned out gargoyles, satyrs, orgiasts, maniacs. Now and then a Job or a Hamlet turned up—or maybe a Roman coin.

Tony Bring took it all with extraordinary calm. Let them spin their opium dreams. Let them talk. They couldn't go to Paris on a shoestring. As for their becoming wealthy overnight—fiddlesticks! If only they made enough to meet the rent when it came due. If they could only keep their stomachs from growling. Hildred talked in carload lots, to be sure, but that was her way. Nothing more than thyroid effervescence.

Toward three or four in the morning Vanya would usually steal out in her overalls and snoop around for milk bottles and bags of buns which the tradesmen left at people's doors. The few hours that remained for sleep they would spend in tossing about, in hurling recriminations, in patching things up. Thoroughly exhausted, her nerves on end, sobbing, weeping, cursing him one moment and surrendering herself the next, Hildred would at last fall asleep in his arms and lie there like a stone. Sometimes she awoke with a fright and cried out—"Oh, it's you!" And then she would beg him to desist, tell him he was cruel, that he was killing her.

"But what were you dreaming of just now?"

"God, I don't know . . . don't ask me such questions. I'm dead, I tell you."

And while he struggled to piece out her dreams, while he

reviewed swiftly all the lies and intrigues that surrounded her, suddenly Vanya would be heard closing the door of her room. Her shadow passed and repassed the heavy stained-glass door. What was she doing out there, that long-maned devil? What new conspiracy was she hatching? As if to protect Hildred from some evil spirit he would seize her and smother her in his arms. And again there would come that nightmarish expression and Hildred would cry out—"O Jesus, leave me alone, will you?"

"But listen, Hildred, don't you hear her?"

"You'll drive me crazy if this keeps up much longer."

"And what about me—do you think I'm getting fat on it?"

"For God's sake, what do you want of me?"

"You know what I want . . . I want you to get rid of her."

"If you talk that way I'll run away . . . I swear I can't stand it any longer."

"But listen, Hildred . . . you say you love me . . . you say you'll do anything for me . . ."

"Yes, but not that!"

"Why not?"

"Because I won't."

"You won't because you're mad . . . you're a son-of-a-bitch . . . you're crazy! I ought to beat the —— out of you."

"Tony . . . Tony! God, what things you say!" She falls on him and suffocates him with kisses. She smooths his brow and runs her hand through his hair. "Tony, my God, how can you talk like that? You're ill. You need a rest. Tony, don't you know that I love you? What would I do without you? Do you want to destroy me?"

"But I'm not mad . . . I mean it. I mean every word of it."

"Oh, Tony, you can't mean it. You're ill. You're ill."

4

EVERYBODY ON pins and needles. Everybody out of sorts,
touchy, jumpy, irritable. Supersensitive. Like a man com-
plaining of cold feet after his legs have been amputated.
Vanya, the Stoic, remarking to Tony Bring one day—"It's
good for you, this suffering . . . it'll improve your writing."

His writing! A pleasant way that was of twitting him about
his slothfulness. The great book whose synopsis had required
sheets and sheets of wrapping paper was no more. Gone up
the flue, with the chairs and whatnot. One could always start
another book, of course. Hadn't Carlyle rewritten his *History
of the French Revolution* when the manuscript was lost? But he
wasn't a Carlyle. Nevertheless, something was gathering
again in his crop. There were scraps of paper and little
notebooks—a sort of Sherwood Anderson nonsense, except
that there was no wandering from flop to flop, no brewery
jobs, no tossing things out of the second-floor window.

Or was it just another way of killing time? One could read
just so much of Spengler and Proust and then there was an
end to it. Joyce too gave one indigestion. In France there
were clever fellows who used the needle every once in a
while. A new book every six months—with illustrations too.

No limits to their fecundity. But in America, somehow, a cocaine atmosphere wouldn't produce literature. America was producing gunmen and beer barons. Literature was being left to women. Everything was left to woman, except womanhood.

What was he scribbling anyway? And why did he have to go to the Caravan to make his notes? Vanya was getting all wrought up about it. If he were thinking of writing a book about her he'd better watch his step. One could bring suit against people for—she didn't know what exactly. Hildred too was urging him to be careful. Heavens, but they were squeamish—and he hadn't written a line yet. Good, nevertheless. Maybe the old cow would really get panicky and bump herself off. She was getting so uneasy nowadays that she hung a knife and a hammer on her door. What was she doing that for? Was she trying to egg him on?

The drama didn't amuse Hildred anymore. She was fagged out. Playing the hostess all day and at night carving wooden legs or dyeing wigs. As for the lord and master, he couldn't even drive a nail in straight. All he did was scribble notes, or think up new arguments to drive them all crazy. No, it couldn't go on much longer—for Hildred. She was worn out, exhausted. Too exhausted even to pretend to make love. And the lord and master—why, he was wide awake when they went to bed. Naturally, since he hadn't done anything all day except to wash the dishes and sweep the floor. Even that was too much for him. It interfered with his scribbling.

There were times now, when they'd gone to bed, that he got up and went for a walk. Hildred didn't even stir when he climbed over her. She was dead to the world.

It was getting to be a habit. He couldn't fall asleep anymore unless he had taken his walk. One night—night? It was almost dawn. He had been walking along the waterfront, turning things over. Deeply engrossed, he wandered into the narrow, canyoned street just back of the warehouses. A deathlike stillness, shattered now and then by the blast of a tugboat. Suddenly there was a shout followed by the sound of scuffling feet. He turned sharply and caught a glancing blow in the neck. The next moment he was in the gutter, rolling over and over. When he got to his feet there was a man standing against the wall. "Come here, you ———!" He began to run. "Stop, you bastard, or you'll be sorry!" He quickened his pace. He was running as fast as his legs would carry him. Then bango! There was a shot and he heard a dull splatter against the wall. He almost collapsed. For a moment there was again the deathlike stillness. And then there came the familiar sound of a nightstick pounding the pavement. That frightened him even more. Supposing the damned fools took it into their heads . . . it was like them to fire away at the first thing they saw. . . .

When he got back to the house he sat down in a chair and began to pant. He was wet and limp. He removed his things slowly, with great effort. He got into bed and lay there trembling. Hildred was lying there like a log. He dozed off. His feet were sticking out of the window. A man came along with an ax and chopped them off; he buried the stumps in the snow which covered the grass plot and then it began to rain and the rain tickled the frozen stumps but he couldn't get out of the window to drag the stumps inside because the window was barred. A car drove up and three men jumped out with shotguns; they rested the guns on the railing and began to spray the window. The window was full of holes through

which the sun poured in; it was tantalizing to lie there with
the sun in your eyes and your feet stuck in the grass plot. He
was walking. So then his feet must have been restored. He
was walking again between the high walls back of the warehouses. And his feet were firmly glued to his legs, because he
was running. Back of him was a mob armed with scythes and
shotguns. And as he ran the walls started closing in on him.
At the end of the street there was just a bare streak of light, as
if a curtain were parted. It was growing thinner and thinner.
He had to turn and edge between the walls. The walls were
scraping his shins. A shot rang out, and then another, and another . . . a grand fusillade. The bullets flattened out above his
head, ricocheted from wall to wall, and dropped like stars at
his feet. There were cries of "Stop! Stop!" but he wriggled on,
stumbling, ducking, scraping his shins and elbows. Suddenly
the walls opened up, moved back like automatic doors, and
the sky burst forth with a tremendous, blinding light. "Saved!
Saved!" he cried. But there, barring the way, all dressed in
gleaming armor, stood a body of foot soldiers with long,
piercing spears thrust forward. Behind him the mob charging
with shouts and curses on their lips. He could hear their
scythes clattering against the walls, almost feel their breath
upon him. A fear so great came over him that he was paralyzed, rooted to the spot. Feebly he tried to raise his hands.
"See . . . see!" he murmured weakly, "I surrender." The
growl ceased. There was a moment of deep, shattering silence. Then, stiff as automatons, the men with the huge,
outthrust spears advanced. When they were almost on top of
him they halted. Slowly they drew back their huge, mailed
arms. "I give up! I give up!" he cried frantically, and as the
words left his mouth—perhaps they were never heard—

there came a blinding rain, a sharp, cruel rain of spears plunged deep and quivering. "Jesus, they've killed me!" he screamed.

When he opened his eyes Hildred was bending over him with a towel in her hands. She looked so sad and gentle. There were tears in her eyes. "What is it?" he asked, and then he saw that there was blood on the towel.

At breakfast he told them what had happened. They looked at him unbelievingly. "What the devil!" he said. "What do you think happened, then?" It was queer the way they regarded him. Hildred looked glum, ravaged. Vanya had put on her Barrymore smile.

"Do you think I tried to pull the Dutch act?"

Vanya was still smiling. "You tried, all right," her smile seemed to say, "but you didn't have the guts."

He looked down at his plate. There were no tragedies anymore, there were only disappointments. He was failing them. He was not a *romantic*, as Vanya used to say. A man who didn't get himself killed when he had everything to die for was a disappointment. A man like that would go on living even if you stuck his feet in the grass plot. He would go on living because he hadn't brains enough to die. It didn't require guts so much as imagination. He was living an amputated life. His imagination had been removed. And without imagination a man could live forever, even though he be a man no longer, even though he have no arms nor legs—as long as there were pieces left that you could sew together and throw in a wheelchair.

5

THE PLACE looks like a toy shop that has just been sacked. Arms and legs lying around, monsters in velour jackets, Neros with green wigs sprawled out on the floor like drunken sailors. Overproduction. Unemployment. All hands out hunting for grub, for cigarettes, firewood. Hildred, sadly discouraged, goes to the cinema frequently and sits in the dark to collect her thoughts. No telling what time they'll come these days. But midnight is sure to find them in the cafeteria on Sheridan Square, the same old joint where Willie Hyslop and his gang used to congregate, where they still meet, to be sure, but not with the enthusiasm and frequency as of yore. So it's here at Lorber's that Vanya and Hildred come after midnight to shake someone down for a little chicken feed. The same old gang—Toots and Ebba, Iliad and her mother, bull-dykers, pimps, poets, painters and painters' whores. . . . Amy, too, drops in once in a while, usually with a shanty on her eye, a gift from that connoisseur of anatomies Homer Reed, him who isn't content with an ordinary bun on, but must needs stretch it out for a year at a time. And then there's Jake. . . . Every few minutes someone pops in to ask where Jake is. And if Jake's there, everything's Jake, as they say.

Who's Jake? Well, Jake is a locksmith—but then that doesn't tell us a thing about him, about his temperament, his great heart, his roguish ways. A Maecenas, would be better . . . a Maecenas with a small *m*. He's a bit of an artist, too, this Jake the Maecenas. That is to say, he keeps a studio hard by—a studio equipped with everything an artist would require. Which means a velvet jacket as well. When he has need of a model—there are always plenty to be had at Lorber's—Jake picks up the check, pays for it, and there you are. Besides being acknowledged an artist he is also considered a good meal ticket. Since it is always the same thing he paints—perhaps painting is too dignified a term for the daubs he makes—Jake economizes by using the same canvas over and over. Vanya, who never had any scruples about posing in the nude, is one of the models Jake knows by heart.

There are other philanthropists to be encountered here also. There is a sea captain and his first mate, for example, and a wizened old fellow with a sea-green beard who used to chop tickets in the subway; there is a chess player named Roberto and a chiropractor who, among other things, has mastered the art of jujitsu. And there is Leslie, the pimply-faced gawk, who has a crush on Vanya and is now driving a taxi. Already quite a nucleus of potential benefactors. It is only a question of keeping them apart, of playing one against the other. The ticket-chopper, for instance, would willingly mortgage his property to help the little ladies along, but he insists that the raven-haired Roberto be gotten out of the way. A droll sort, this venerable ticket-chopper. Writes the most touching letters, in a medieval script. Signed Ludwig. Poor Ludwig's letters are passed around from table to table amid gales of laughter, even while the poor fish is present, perhaps at the very moment when he is reaching down into his long jeans to peel off a five-spot.

Now and then, just to prove that they really have a *domicile fixe*, one of the knight-errants is invited over to the "morgue." If it is a question of laying in supplies, Jake is a good man to corral. Scarcely does he remove his hat when Vanya suddenly recalls that there is no food in the house. A moment of mock embarrassment, perplexity. Then Jake, innocently: "Why didn't you tell me you were hungry at the restaurant?" But they weren't hungry then. "Well, let's go out and buy some food. We'll eat here, eh?" Fine. Nothing finer. And forthwith they take Jake by the hand and lead him to an expensive delicatessen store where one can purchase caviar, pâté de foie gras, Maxwell House coffee, black pumpernickel, and other delicatesses. They return with enough provisions to last a week. Jake may even reflect thus aloud.

After he has been fed, and treated to one of his own cigars, Hildred is sure to complain that it is getting stuffy. She will go to the window and, after opening it slightly, pull the shade halfway. And lo and behold, a moment later the bell rings. And there, standing at the door, is their old friend Tony Bring. Why what are you doing at this hour? He was just passing, to be sure, and seeing the light in the window he thought he'd say hello. Though, truth to tell, saying hello was quite an effort for him—the muscles of his face almost paralyzed from the cold. Just passing by, he was. No mention of the two hundred and seventy-three times he had "passed by" before the shade was raised. . . .

But when the sea captain and his first mate are invited over Tony Bring exhibits an unexpected stubbornness. It isn't the cold any longer that he objects to, because he has change

enough to sit in an armchair at Bickford's. It's just stubbornness. Or was it, perhaps, that he didn't quite trust these bluff,
honest, seafaring fellows? At any rate, he refuses to be
budged. Insists on locking himself in Vanya's room. . . .

AND SO, while the gourmandizing went on, he lay in the dark
listening to the water gurgling while he tried to piece together
the fragments of conversation which drifted to his ears. At
times it actually appeared to him that there was no conversation going on at all, but it was explained afterward that these
lapses were given over to a silent scrutiny of Vanya's poems.
That he should have dared to breathe such nasty insinuations, however, called for some acidulous comments. It was
Hildred who declared that a sailor could be as much of a
gentleman as the next fellow, perhaps more of a one.

But shortly after this visit, with the usual contradictoriness
which attaches itself to human events, the two of them came
home in a grand huff. It was after an evening at the theater
with the gallant tars.

"What do you think those bastards tried to do?" It was
Hildred who exploded thus, no sooner than she had opened
the door.

In that enfeebled state to which his imagination had been
reduced Tony Bring confessed that he hadn't the slightest
idea what could have happened.

"They tried to kiss us—can you imagine that? We were in
the cab, talking about"—she turned to Vanya—"what was it
we were discussing again?"

And Vanya, with a sickly grin, responded: "You were
trying to explain what sadism meant."

"Yes, that's it—sadism. . . . I'm trying to knock it into their thick skulls when all of a sudden I feel an arm creeping around my neck. It was that dirty old fool, the captain. He said I had to give him just one little kiss. . . ."

She paused a moment to observe the reaction the "little kiss" would provoke, but as Tony Bring betrayed not even a mild astonishment, she added with a fury a little too ardent— "I gave him a good crack in the jaw!"

Vanya couldn't refrain from tittering. That seemed to incense Hildred even more than the insulting behavior of the gentlemen in the taxicab.

"What's the matter with you?" she cried.

"Oh, nothing," said Vanya, and turned her face away.

"And that's all there was to it?" said Tony Bring. He couldn't understand why the fuss about it. He looked at Vanya—her face was slipping.

"I don't see what you're laughing for," Hildred exclaimed angrily. "Didn't I slap his face? Didn't I? And *you* . . . what did *you* do?"

A scene was precipitated during which the word *slut* was bandied back and forth. He listened to them in amazement. Hildred calling her dear sick genius, her princess, a slut! Finally Vanya retreated to her room, slammed the door in Hildred's face, and locked herself in. After a time they heard her sobbing.

"For God's sake, go in there and quiet her," said Tony Bring. "I can't stand that noise . . . you'd think she was having her throat cut."

But Hildred wouldn't move. There were some things, she let it be known, that were unforgivable.

What things? he asked himself. What was the meaning of

all this? *Just a little kiss* . . . ? That couldn't be it. What *really*
happened? His imagination was running wild. It would all
leak out in due time, but. . . . Meanwhile he could hear
Vanya sobbing, sobbing as if her heart would break. And
then, just when it seemed impossible to endure another
moment, the sobbing ceased, and there was a long, sinister
silence. Maybe she'll do something desperate, he thought to
himself, and his mind ran on like a clock—police, court,
headlines, cemetery, suicide, despair, ennui, frustration. If
she'd only do it! Do it, you bastard! He was startled by a
blood-curdling yell quickly followed by a din and clatter as
if shoes were being thrown around. Hildred sprang to her
feet and, rushing to Vanya's door, pounded away with her
two fists. "Vanya . . . Vanya dear, open the door. *Please*,
Vanya . . . I want to speak to you. . . ." There was a moment
of intense silence and then a volley of curses. "Vanya . . .
Vanya! I'm sorry. . . . Forgive me! *Please*, Vanya . . . *please*
open the door!"

They heard her thrashing about, stumbling against the
furniture, back and forth, back and forth, like a maniac. Then
her queer, mad voice caroling away like a drunken angel, an
angel with a Russian accent, an angel with a Victrola in her
gizzard and the spring running down, sliding through all the
registers of the human voice, running down, down, like rain
falling into the sewers. . . .

Tony Bring's disappointment was violent and bitter.
Fireworks—that's all it amounted to. In the morning she'd
be clamoring for strawberries and cream. He worked himself
up to such a pitch of fury that he was almost on the point of
ripping his own guts out. If only the door hadn't been locked!
If he could have been in there with her and handed her the

bread knife when she was bellowing like a stuck pig! He felt humiliated.

HE WAS standing on the threshold of Vanya's room with a broom in his hand. Somehow, every time he visited this wing of the morgue he was seized with an insane desire to lay about with shovel and pitchfork, to clean out the manure and stomp down a fresh bed of straw. "Here lives a horse," he growled. "A horse that is not a horse but an acrobat evacuating poetry. An animal that steeps itself in the mire of its own dung. A frisky brute that adds pictures to the wall with each whisk of its tail. Not a horse, either, but a sea cow with a yellow tail, a lazy, herbivorous beast that poisons itself with tobacco. With its wet, cumbersome fins it sprawls over the desk under the toilet box and sucks inspiration from the gurgle of the drains. . . ."

Everything about the place smelled of decay, of depravity. It was here in this foul, moist den that she wrestled with the demons of her dreams, or rolled off the cot when the walls heaved and bulged. Here, when she got drunk, that she curled up like a fetus and lapped up the ashes of her cigarettes. Here that her friends came and, standing on the cot in their dirty shoes, expounded their moth-eaten theories of art, or pinned bloomers on her fleshy nudes, or added a missing nose or a foot. A dirty womb of a place, spewing darkness and poison, slippery and lurid as the opalescent mucus of Michelet.

Broom in hand he went from room to room. A dungeon! A stinking oubliette! Living with these two was like living with a double-headed monster. He lit a candle and held it to the walls, moved about from one image to another. Sword swallowers, nymphs with varicose veins, dryads and hamadryads sucking the moon, dime museums, skeletons with crazy hats, fountains that bled like gems, Leda and the swan, vegetables that spoke . . .

A pale light trickled in as he drew aside the heavy burlap curtains. It was day outside! The day! One day after another, dribbling away in confusion, marked neither by beginning nor end. Like the tides following after the moon they rolled up, one upon another, now swelling to a flood of furious activity, now dropping to a stagnant ebb. And it was in this drift that one was said to *live*. On the surface of this ceaseless drift forms arose, brilliant and energized; for an infinitesimal fraction of time life imparted to them a flash and poise; in the glitter of their passing something like a somber significance attached to them. But like a meteor sweeping through cold space they were gone; like dead sea life, inert, extinct, they dropped below the molten surface, through the deep gloom of terrifying depths, and deposited their skeletons on the floor of the universe. In violence and chaos, with futility and despair, rising from inchoate blackness and slime only to fall again.

He juggled the candle back and forth. Like a fiery tongue the flame licked the walls, staining a delicate arm with veins, making torsos dance and muscles quiver. Spots of color leaped out at him; they were like the evil traits that one surprises on the face of a friend in sleep.

6

IT WAS toward midnight when he ascended the steps that led to the little balcony of Paul & Joe's. It was a Sunday night. The balcony was jammed with sailors parading arm in arm with handsome young faggots who lisped and rolled their eyes deliriously. In the hallway, packed like a subway train at rush hour, women were embracing one another, whites and blacks promiscuously. The air reeked with perfumes. The place was in an uproar. He made his way to the basement, where, almost in the center of the room, sat Hildred surrounded by a clump of wasted-looking females among whom were Toots and Ebba, and Iliad and her mother. They were drooped over the tables in slovenly attitudes, all of them talking at once, none of them concerned apparently with the riot going on. They look wilted, he said to himself, as he walked up to the table and patted Hildred on the shoulder.

She looked up at him dumbfounded.

"I'd like to have a word with you," he said. At once the babble ceased.

Excusing herself, Hildred rose and went to the dressing room, followed by Vanya, who glared at him vengefully. He took a seat beside a fat Norwegian girl with whom Hildred had been talking. She seemed to be the only one who did not resent his intrusion. Despite the sleepy expression in her eyes she betrayed an uncommonly alert mind, an almost insolent directness. At the same time there was something ridiculous about her—her big, flabby breasts hung beneath her stiff shirt like frying pans. She inquired if he had known Hildred and Vanya very long. The conversation was interrupted. Two bristling Lesbians at opposite ends of the room suddenly jumped to their feet and began singing to each other, the one in a deep baritone, the other in a falsetto poisoned with drink. The performance was no sooner concluded than a young Viking got up and with the voice of an angel warbled "My Little Gray Home in the West." Then a sailor rose and sang a smutty song, whereupon the Norwegian girl asked very bluntly and coldly how long Hildred had been taking dope. He looked at her in amazement. Then Toots and Ebba broke in. They couldn't understand, they said, why Vanya permitted a person like Hildred to tyrannize over her. Anyone could see that Hildred was empty. It was Vanya who had all the personality, the brains. Iliad's mother put in a word too. She had no use for Hildred. She was suspicious of her, though what she was suspicious of she didn't make clear. Ebba said that Hildred was a fake through and through. She wasn't really interested in Vanya—she was just using her. If anyone asked her opinion, what Hildred wanted was *a man*. "You mean to say . . . ?" exclaimed Iliad's mother, but she stopped suddenly when she saw the look on her daughter's face. Here Minna, the Norwegian girl, came to life again. There was a sly twinkle in her eye, a malicious twinkle that had been hidden by the film of scum which seemed to gather in her eyes at will. "For all you know," she said, "Hildred may be married. If she's not married, she's in love with someone . . . some man. Vanya's not the only string to her fiddle." This was greeted with a burst of laughter followed by uncontrollable mirth when Iliad attempted to say that Hildred was a very sweet person, that she had never been anything but a good friend to her, and so on.

THEY WERE lying in bed. He refused to explain why he had come for her, why he had dragged her home and not a word out of his trap. All he did was to mumble some gibberish— "men with colored shirts . . . athletes with bull necks"— gibberish . . . gibberish. Every once in a while he turned over and said, "The letter . . . the letter wouldn't go down the toilet," and then he'd fall back again on his broken phrases. She pretended to go to sleep, she even snored in her sleep, but still he kept on mumbling. "The letter . . . the letter that wouldn't go down the toilet . . . strictly personal . . . sacred . . ." She snored harder now.

When he had stopped his mumbling and she felt quite sure that he was asleep she slipped out of bed and fumbled through his coat pockets. He was lying there peacefully with hands folded on his breast. She lit a match to make sure that his eyes were tightly closed. Then, on tiptoe, she made a beeline for the bathroom. "Fine!" murmured Tony Bring in his sleep. "Fine! Let them hide it again. Words that refuse to go down the toilet always bob up again."

Her mind must have been at ease, because when she returned to bed she fell asleep at once. Her mind was always at ease after she had been to the bathroom. But this time it must have been quite a surprise to the little nun in her cell to have a special delivery handed her. Would she remember the hand-writing of her pre-Romanoff period? "My Sodom and Go-morrah!" That was how it started. "You that toss green lips so lightly. Men with colored shirts, athletes with bull necks . . . lovers always parting at these heavy doors. The river has a current and dead rats float away quickly, but I am not a dead rat. There is a revolver but the bullets always stick. I did not succeed in committing suicide . . . but I love you, Hildred. I love you terribly." (A terrible Platonic love, no doubt, com-ing from Sodom to Gomorrah.) "Hildred, you would be a rare delicate pervert (pardon!) if all this infernal chaos which surrounds you were removed. Please, don't you see what you contain?" Since that time, of course, the delicate little pervert had probably looked into the jeweled casket of her soul and found what she contained. He thought of Minna, the Nor-wegian girl, with the frying pans hanging from her neck. How had she managed to pry open the lid of this satin-lined casket and what had she found? Were there skeletons inside as well as athletes with bull necks? And where was the husband amid all this incense and perfumery? Was he depos-ited there, too, along with the colored shirts and the bullets that always stuck?

She was lying close to him, relaxed, inert, her face turned to his in peaceful trance. Her breath was a little boozy. But she was beautiful . . . beautiful. Not a trace of evil, of lies, or drugs. Innocence. Sublime innocence. *I love you, Hildred, I love you terribly.* The miracle was that people didn't prostrate themselves at her feet, in the street. Miracle that she was flesh and blood, and not a statue, a flower, or a precious stone. *A rare, delicate pervert. . . .* He looked at her brow, so smooth, so peaceful, so absolutely impenetrable. A bundle of mystery, even to herself. What lay behind that wall of flesh and bone? Could he ever hope to know what was going on there? Supposing, in a moment of deep contrition, she were to say—"I will tell you *everything.*" Even then he would never know. He would know only what she wanted him to know, nothing more.

So obsessed did he become by the thought of his helplessness that at last he closed his eyes and surrendered himself to a flight of fantastic, wanton cruelty. Like a cold, searching vivisectionist, he saw himself bending over her with scalpel, stripping away the flesh from the brain, sawing through the bone with steady hand to expose the soft, dull-gray convolutions, the delicate, palatable tangle of mystery which no one could unravel. A cold, mirthless laugh escaped him— the laugh that is heard only in solitude. The laugh which a dog might give vent to if he were trained to understand human jokes. He repeated to himself empty formulas from the joke books of the pundits. Everything in the universe they could explain, including God Almighty, but themselves no. They poked around in entrails, boiled invisible microbes, weighed the imponderable, extracted the juices of anger and jealousy, analyzed the composition of planets no bigger to the eye than a pinhead—but the most difficult thing for them to do was to admit that they knew nothing. Or, if they admitted it, their language was so complicated, so grandiloquent, that it was impossible to believe them. No one could say so much about nothing as the man who pretended to know nothing.

With this babble on his lips he fell into a profound slumber in which he dreamed that he was hanging by his feet from the roof of a freight car. He could see only the floor and the cages of the men beside him. The car was filled with cages, man-sized circular cages suspended from the ceiling. They were all hanging by the feet. When the train swerved the cages collided, made a faint, ringing noise. The conversation was upside down, too, or perhaps it was because they were all crazy that it seemed so. When they arrived in front of the asylum the cages were brought out one by one: they were marked FRAGILE. There they were, all neatly docketed and swinging by the legs. One labeled "phagomania" inquired if they were going to be fed this way, upside down, and the attendant replied, "Certainly, why not? If you can talk upside down you can eat upside down." Whereupon the cages were placed in a circle and a beautiful white horse was led out. Strange thing about the horse was that it had a peacock's tail. Stranger still was that it pranced about on its hind legs and spoke English to them. Going up to each cage, the horse would make a bow and ask, in perfect equine English—"Are you balanced or unbalanced?" Such a question! No one would respond to this nonsense. And so they were carried off, each and every one of them, and placed in a refrigerator to cool off. And no one could determine anymore whether he was balanced or unbalanced. It was chilly in the refrigerator and the cages swung like pendulums. Time passed. Ice-cold time. It was a different kind of time than they had ever experienced before. It was ice-cold time, without divisions and without arrest. A circular, prenatal time, without springs, or pulse, or flux. . . .

Part 6

1

———————◆———————

THE END. All things come to an end where they begin again assuming a circle or a dog chasing its tail or eternity cognized which is incomprehensible and indefeasible. The end is a rabbit licking moonlight off the pavement, revolvers clicking automatically where the spine flattens into a bony globe. The end is the beginning of a circle before the periphery becomes paralyzed and coagulates into points which never existed and could not now exist were there no blackboards and what makes blackboards. The end is when every drawer has been ransacked and all that one needs can be put in a handkerchief or when you don't need initials in your hat anymore and the size is an empty equation. The compass points four ways and you can travel horizontally or vertically because it is all illusion—tickets, depots, destination, mileage, speed. When you say good-bye that's the end of it, a peculiar, unfinished end like a tapeworm feeding on itself. An end that comes to a lump in the throat or a sob, wheels grinding, soot, farms, faces, blank, blankness, faces, farms, memories, musk of memory, wheels grinding, bullets clicking, too late, everything too late, change, change your mind, stay, jump, go back, mist, farms, faces, blank, blankness.

177

He had no more than shut the door when she flew upstairs to the telephone. "He's on his way . . . he's coming . . . he's going away. Yes, he wants to say good-bye. good-bye. I'm coming. I'll be there in a little while. good-bye. good-bye."

Eye to eye, fire to fire. Blood-red ice and black perfume. Moon goddess and moon fire. The smoke of vanished kisses. Harp bleeding its green music, poppies floating in a cold sea. The roundness of the beginning, the end like a navel. Craters flowing with blood-red ice, hemispheres of warm milk, swan's down and meat of olives.

The miracle was good-bye and that ends it. Farms, faces, wheels grinding. I love you terribly don't you see what you contain? Black chunks of earth flying skyward you that toss green lips so lightly.

The remembrance of things was in her touch, incorruptible egg that precedes and endures, memory unsponged and glowing with a last light. The ripple of her loins secreted in blood, her breasts tipped with melancholy, the drugged smoke and passion of her lies laced with scars and fang-whorl, dyke on dyke of bleeding harps, of kisses suffocated with poppies and melancholy, of youth run out, womb turned, strings snapping with death music, music of night written on sand and the sand spangled with star and wave illumining the scorpion's nest.

A thousand years of melancholy lay between them and she had no answer to make. What was there to answer if life were a poem, the drug and incense of endless yesterdays and tomorrows. Under the table their knees touched. Under how many tables knees and hands, skeletons articulated with

178

love, things that walk automatically and touch, pollen, roots digging down, fibers and vertebrae, green juices, the wind soughing and things crawling in the night making no sound. Stir and movement, wings folding, the prick of light without heat, worlds sighing inaudibly and bones whitening and dust coming to life.

His whole life was hanging by a thread. In her hand was a paper covered with words which she would read and rearrange in her mind. There was a physics and a chemistry of words; there was an electrolysis of language, thought raised to symbol, vested and divested, polarized by blood, anchored in instinct, veering with the moon its ebb and tide through the monotonous mad cycle of imagined flesh and life, prison-bar and window of sky, songburst and delirium. She would take them one by one, the intangible inner harmony of cathode and vortex and the sweet visible substance of molecular growth, she would take them and arrange them dynamically in script of living.

Either she would let him go or she would beg him to remain. Not enough to say—"Don't go!" Not nearly enough. No, something tremendous would have to occur. She would have to get down on her knees and beg and implore. Once, before there was any thought of questions and answers, she had gotten down on her knees to him, in the street. She had called him her "god." Since then other gods had come to life. The great god had given way to little gods. But there is only one god. It can never be otherwise since by virtue of definition god is god.

The time for tremendous things had passed. "Go for a little while—but come back to me!" Those were her very words. The life, then, had gone out of her. She was making herself a

fulcrum and there was to be a stale, flat equilibrium, a simu-
lacrum of living, passion reduced to geometry. *Go for a little
while.* . . . She was standing in slime, her eyes wide open, and
where she saw angels there were albatrosses. The sky still
fluttered with wings but these were not angels that fell exhausted at her feet.

SUDDENLY VANYA sailed in—grazed in, rather. A ferryboat
shoving into the slip sidewise. She was breathless, squeaking
a little. The tide was running strong. There was the sound of
wood splintering and the engine going reverse.

"He's not really going, is he?" she demanded.

"Yes," said Hildred, "but only for a little while."

"No! I'll go instead. I won't let him go."

She spoke excitedly, repeated herself, dropped into her
strange Russian accent. Hildred, deadly calm, listened with
eyes frozen; behind the mask terror turning to bile. Her mind
turned over like a turbine.

The idea was so simple, so monstrously direct and brutal,
that it numbed them. Up to this moment they had been
hobbling along on crutches; suddenly they were commanded
to throw them away. Not only that, but they were ordered to
walk to the edge of the precipice and hurl themselves over.
No warning, no preparation. Not even a drop of holy water to
usher in the miracle, not a bone to touch, nor even the smell
of a plague. Husband and wife sat there with knees touching:
they faced each other like rival cities exhausted by centuries
of strife. It was as if some horrible deception had been prac-
ticed on them, as if peace had been won without slaughter,
as if nature herself had intervened, had opened the earth

between them and nullified their antagonism. It was altogether unnatural and against all human instinct to walk away from a complicated flesh-and-blood problem like a mesmerist who leaves the stage with his subject poised in midair, stiff, cataleptic, ridiculously helpless. Tomorrow a whole continent might slip into the sea: it was not to say whether it was just or unjust. But if a woman, giving birth to a monster, should take it upon herself to dash the child's brains out, that was another matter, that was a crime against nature, or against society, something whether just or unjust punishable by law. Society had so complicated the relations between men, had so enmeshed the individual with laws and creeds, with totems and taboos, that man had become something unnatural, something apart from nature, a phenomenon which nature herself had created, but which she no longer controlled.

HE WALKED down lower Broadway with Vanya and over the Brooklyn Bridge. She insisted on carrying his valise; gratefully she carried it, like a porter who is proud of the privilege to accompany a great explorer to his hotel, so proud, indeed, that he would feel insulted if offered a tip.

Hildred was to come home as soon as she was through.

They arrived at the house, the great explorer and his porter, and shoved the valise in a corner. Now what? Would the great explorer like some tea and jam, could she light his cigarette for him? She undid his shoes and helped him into a pair of warm house slippers, threw her bathrobe over him, and adjusted the lights. A thousand uninstructed delicacies. . . .

Hildred would return soon. She whispered to him, like a nurse saying "Shhhh! Mother will soon be here." A crime to feed babies from the bottle. What a child needs is a mother's breast. Modern mothers have no breasts, or else they strangle them. Nevertheless, a mother is a mother; a bottle can never take the place of a breast.

In the interim the baby amused the nurse by inventing fairy tales. . . .

Once there was a queen with golden hair and ebony buttocks. She came from the Tropic of Capricorn, which is below the equator. Her tongue was of quicksilver and she worshiped strange gods. They were of convenient size and weight, her gods; she collected them, when she wished to amuse herself, and hid them in a casket. Sometimes she wore them around her neck, like beads. Often, when she went for a stroll, she would say to herself—"There is still room in the casket for another god." Whereupon, at the sound of a god-like tread, she would prostrate herself at the feet of a stranger and cry: "You are my god! I will worship you—always . . . always!" And because she was too impulsive to heed closely, she would discover on occasion that she had made a mistake, that she had given her devotion to a cow or a grampus.

"WHERE'S VANYA?" cried Hildred. She spoke in a strange voice, as if her diaphragm were afire, as if she were belching smoke. Though she looked everywhere—under the bathtub, under the toilet box, under the sink—there was no Vanya. But all her things were there, including the dirty wash that she had thoughtfully tucked under the bed. And the Count was there, lying in the corner like an old mandolin. And there were arms and legs lying about, and sleeves, and wigs that had been dipped in heliotrope. It was like a laboratory in which an experiment was going on—an unfinished experiment. A home that could combine all the elements of poem and laboratory—such a home leaves nothing to be desired except music and children. Of the two, music was perhaps the more difficult to lure. There was that old mandolin, the Count, to be sure, and there was the music box in the zenana which would tinkle melodiously as long as a pipe remained. And there was the blood-red harp which bled green notes, which when all the strings quivered gave forth a symphony of Sicilian moons. The children would come in due time. Vanya, in her drunken moments, feeling her bladder distended, would promise to bring forth a blond superman— though by all the laws of heredity genius rarely produced anything but mediocrities. Of all the dreams that invaded Hildred's slumber this one of the wise, blond baby with the dash of septentrional vigor in its blood was the most bizarre and astonishing. It was born over and over again, always with a full set of teeth and a miraculous tongue. It lisped slightly, not because of any malformation, but out of sheer perversity. But this was nothing considering the marvels it uttered. They were not words which fell from its lips, but jewels spilling from a casket. Now and then, amid the cascade, bones dropped—never very many, hardly enough, one would say, to make a good-sized skeleton. . . .

TOWARD MORNING the telephone rang. Hildred slipped into a kimono and ran upstairs. She spoke so softly that it was like a caress. He could scarcely hear her though he stood on tiptoes at the foot of the staircase. "I can't . . . I can't" was all he could make out.

"She's terribly drunk," said Hildred when she got back to bed. "I could hardly understand her."

"Where is she, then?"

"I don't know," said Hildred.

"Well what did she want?"

"She wanted me to bring her home."

"How could you fetch her if you don't know where she is?"

"That's just it."

"That's too bad!" said Tony Bring. "She's going to the dogs."

So heartily did Hildred laugh at this—and it was seldom she laughed at anything he said—that one of the veins in her neck blew up and remained inflated for days.

2

Everybody knew who the nightingale of Lesbos was, but it was Vanya who discovered that she was the eightieth asteroid as well as a hummingbird with fiery tail. There were poems to the eightieth asteroid and to pigeons, those ditokous birds who lay only two eggs in a clutch. Like a purple heron Vanya was preening herself in the swamps and marshes of knowledge. She spoke of delphinoid cetaceans and golden groupers, of asymptotes and parabolas, of Sarvasti who was Science, of batrachians and lapiths. For three whole days she flooded their ears with a hemorrhage on white heartrot. This was a disease usually mentioned only by arboriculturists. Vanya appropriated it. There are diseases and diseases. But this disease had a fascination about it. It was brought on by a destructive species of fungus that attacked the heartwood of various broadleaf trees. Like the grampus, the fake tinder fungus was a killer, only instead of preying upon seals and marine life it attacked trees. A broadleaf tree was absolutely defenseless against the fake tinder fungus. Once the latter effected entrance to the heart of the tree it was all up; injecting bisulfide of carbon through the sawdust openings, or spraying the foliage with arsenate of lead, was of no avail. *It was death from white heartrot!*

It made her positively daffy, this song of corruption, this arboreal saga of death and transfiguration. She behaved like a rotten sloop riding out to a storm. While the wind howled in her brain the maggots were busy below—converting the wood to sawdust. No use trying to stop the wounds with putty. The wounds spread, left big holes in her sides through which you could poke an umbrella.

ARRIVING HOME late one night Tony Bring found Hildred sitting alone, her head buried in her arms. She was sobbing. And Vanya? Vanya was in her room scribbling—laying bluish-green eggs, unblemished, cute as pigeon eggs. There was a drama going on, but which act it was, or what the plot, he couldn't tell. Secretive souls: tight-lipped, loyal as crooks. No tender polyps these, even though ravaged by war. Strange that things should go awry now, just when everyone was employed and Paris nearer than ever. Perhaps something had gone wrong at the art school . . . perhaps Vanya had taken to playing the slut again. It was stupid work, certainly, sitting on a stool with a rag around your breasts, or standing on one leg and dreaming. Who could blame them if they fortified themselves with a little gin? Weary of imitating marble, of inspiring dreams, the nightingale of Lesbos sometimes indulged in hysterics. It was the hysteria of a statue. But when some kind soul had fed her snowflakes she became tractable again, turned to marble, never lost her balance. Leaving the academy she would fly like a hummingbird and spread her fiery tail. It was because of her great swoops that she developed

notalgia, which is a curious word for "pain in the back."
Hildred insisted that she meant nostalgia, but nostalgia was
not the word. It was not homesickness, but a disorder of the
spine that she had contracted. It came from flying, or from
posing as a Winged Victory. Until they fed her snowflakes
there was no relief.

AND TONY Bring—what is he doing for a livelihood? He has
been so quiet lately, so subdued. One would never think, to
see this quiet, sober individual marching home, that he had
been shouting all night at the top of his lungs. He is distinctly
not the sort to raise his voice in the marketplace, or the
subway. At first it sounded more like a whisper when he
opened his mouth. But one can't sell papers by whispering to
people. No, that he learned quickly enough. One had to
develop a stentorian voice, a voice of brass that would rouse
even the dead from their dreams. One had to hustle and
shove, to elbow his way, to bawl louder than the next fellow.
Only thus could one get rid of his load. On Saturday nights
Tony Bring knew what notalgia was—it was curvature of the
spine. Only in his case it didn't come from soaring, for if he
had wings he was unaware of them or they were atrophied.
He felt rather as the snail must feel, crawling along with a
house on its back. And when the snow came and the headlines announced that it was a blizzard it was a blizzard
because blizzards are blizzards. The soft, spineless flakes, in-
nocuous, tasteless, deodorized, carried the message through
the conduits of his nerves and diluted his blood. . . . Though
now he was linked closer than ever with the great metro-
politan press he read nothing but headlines. The headlines

were the dikes erected by addled brains to ward off the flood of print that rose with each edition and threatened to drown the inhabitants. They were written in stench and sweat, they conspired like prostitutes, they screamed with cancerous fury, they poetized and glorified the scrimmage, they crucified the sinners, they embalmed the dead, electrified the dullwitted, roused the constipated from their sodden lethargy. The headlines weighed on his mind, strangled his dreams, broke his back. It was not a body he brought home at night, but a collection of bruises. His dreams were those of the caterpillar before it has learned to fly, of the turtle whose back is pounded by breakers.

BETTER THAN standing on one leg with a towel around your hips was to furnish blood for the needy. The only capital required was health. If one had good health one had good blood and blood was selling at a premium these days. It sold for anywhere from fifteen dollars to one hundred dollars the pint. According to the grade. Supposing, for instance, one had Grade A blood. Of course it wasn't called Grade A, but then that doesn't matter. The point was that if one ate well, drank a glass of port regularly, and kept the intestines free from poisons, one could sell a pint of blood every ten or fifteen days. No need to drum up business, no political influence required, no capital to be invested. Just good, rich, healthy red blood—Grade A preferably—and that's all there was to it.

Now there was in the Village a certain blood donor who knew the game from A to Izzit. He was Grade A, and his wife was on a par with him, speaking of blood quality. They had given away enough blood, between them, to float a battle-ship. And look at them! Fine bloom to their cheeks, fur coats . . . you could see them at the Caravan most any night consuming beefsteaks, dancing with both feet, drunk with blood or loss of blood.

There were hospitals and hospitals in New York, some better than others, from the standpoint of blood donors. A certain Jewish institution was the most generous of all, but then there was a waiting list—a formidable waiting list. Of course, when one got known, when the quality of one's blood acquired a reputation, as it were, one could work his way up. Best to start with a modest institution—with a Presbyterian hospital, or something like that.

But first they had to give specimens. They gave away—absolutely gratis, as samples—ordinary syringefuls. They left their samples all over the city. Hildred had a bad time of it; some amateur punctured her in the wrong place and her arm swelled up and the veins grew black. She swore she was going to lose her arm, but as it turned out, she didn't. And then she had vomiting spells. Even wild strawberries wouldn't stay on her stomach. The only thing that agreed with her was port wine. Port wine was a tonic. She advised everyone to drink port.

There were hospitals that weren't satisfied just to puncture one's arm. Insisted on thoroughgoing examination: heart, lungs, urinalysis, height, weight, Wasserman test, nationality, heredity, etc. One could be insured for fifty thousand dollars with less fuss. And then there were the young bloods with the stethoscopes slung around their necks—they were devils for thoroughness. Even a little thing like a brassiere interfered with their patient, exhaustive inquiries. There were others—tired old duffers—who didn't even ask you to cough. A thoroughly quixotic business, no matter from what angle you viewed it.

And then came the reports! They arrived in the mail like rejection slips from editorial offices. Some were printed, stereotyped forms couched in superpolite language; some were curt and rude, written in longhand—by foreigners or night watchmen. One thing stood out clearly: they were unfit. They were neither Grade A, nor Grade B, nor Grade C, nor Grade D. The good red corpuscles so much in demand at the moment showed a minus sign. Aside from the question of good or bad blood there were other things the matter with them. There were so many things the matter with them that it was only by a miracle they fell short of cancer, dropsy, or syphilis. At the bottom of all their ills lay anemia. Anemia was a sort of white heartrot developed by city organisms, a disease that turned the blood to dishwater. Who could furnish a clean bill of blood in a city like New York? It was all nonsense. They weren't going to have the daylight scared out of them by young rubbernecks with stethoscopes slung around their necks and white trousers creased to a razor's edge. *Undernourished*—that was the answer to the whole problem. More strawberries. More port. Thick juicy steaks with blood-red gravy. The doctors be damned! They were just false alarms. If you had money and you could afford to worry about your health, they'd scare you to death. A millionaire could be kept alive, even if his stomach were cut out. There were men whose tongues had been eaten away by cancer or depravity, yet they were able to go to the dinner table in a tuxedo and feed themselves through an artificial hole. A poor man, if he had only a cough, was allowed to die of neglect. Coughs didn't interest the medical profession much. The druggist took care of coughs and backaches. The progress of medicine was such that it was no longer a science, if science it ever was, but an art. The art of prolonging life— by artificial means. Ah, if there were no rich, what refinements would be lacking, what subtleties, what complexities! In the bodies of the rich disease sprouted luxuriantly. On these refined manure piles what marvelous roses bloomed, what beautiful ulcers! Out of dotards and hyenas the men of science were almost prepared now to make butterflies. Progress ... progress.... A century ago the tree of life was fast rotting away—but today it flourished and would go on flourishing though the trunk were three-quarters cement.

3

ON THE night of Lincoln's birthday there was a blizzard, and between Lincoln's birthday and Washington's birthday it snowed on and off and everything was wrapped in wadding so that even the ash barrels and the garbage cans looked attractive. And while the snow fell things happened, as they do in Russian novels, in the Russian soul where there is God and snow and ice and talk and murder and epilepsy, where history leaves off only to make place for nature, where be it only a room there is space for the biggest drama ever written, space for the invisible host and for all peoples, climates, tongues. On the night of Lincoln's birthday, just before the blizzard fell out of the sky, Hildred stepped out in a velvet suit to mail a letter. She was gone three days and three nights in her velvet suit that had hollow silver balls down the front. There were twenty-six or twenty-seven of them, all empty, and each one veined with cicatrices which, to a microscopic organism endowed with sense of vision, would no doubt appear as the canals on the planet Mars appear to the human eye. In her absence the telephone never rang once, nor did any of the crippled, aged, or demented emissaries of the telegraph company ring the doorbell, present an open-face envelope and an inch and a half of pencil without lead saying "Sign here." The world was wrapped in wadding and the wadding gave out no news.

Tony Bring lay in his bed and Vanya lay in hers. The first day said Vanya aren't you worried and he answered no. On the second day said Vanya what are you going to do and he answered nothing. The third day said Vanya I'm going to notify the police and he made no reply. But instead of notifying the police she went out and got drunk and when she returned she was raving about cathedrals and rats and athletes with bull necks; she even ceased to be original and called herself "an arrow of yearning for the other shore." Toward morning she began to sing off-key and scream and shriek, she got up and held the walls apart with her dirty palms. The Danish sisters rapped on the floor with their shoes. This having no effect, the only thing left to do was to throw a pail of water over her, which was done. Thereupon she slept as calmly as if she were in a straitjacket and Tony Bring examined her toenails, which were long and bent. In the morning Hildred walked in, her eyes glassy, and all the explanation that she offered was that she had met a poet, saying which she tumbled into bed without even removing her velvet suit, which now had only twenty-two or twenty-three balls down the front, all of them empty and each and every one of them veined with cicatrices.

She had a long, long sleep and when she awoke no one knew whether it was seven in the morning or seven at night. She opened the window and collected a bowl of snow. Then she went out and bought food—heaps of food—and said how beautiful it was out of doors. Two things were good for the complexion and two only: a damp climate, such as

England had, and wet snow. No matter what she touched on there was snow on her tongue. Her eyes were still glassy, and though her spirit was bright it was strangely bright, snow-bright, and after she had eaten she vomited and the beautiful glow on her cheeks that had come with the snow disappeared and her skin looked as it had always looked—flour-white, satiny, heavy, languid. With her bright red lips and her bright round eyes she was like a fever-wraith and her talk had fever in it.

From the day the blizzard set in, which was Lincoln's birthday, until Washington's birthday Tony Bring never got out of bed except to go to the bathroom. He was down with hemorrhoids. In a box containing a tube of ointment which Hildred purchased at the druggist they found a description of the malady printed in five languages. The English read as follows:

Hemorroides

Hemorroides are varicous veins produced by the dilatation of the veins of the body rectum. They are due chiefly to constipation and enteritis and can be internal or external. Sometimes itchings accompany the push. The saddle is nearly always painful.

Our Treatment

Avoid in food all that can inflame the system such as spiced food, game, etc.

Eat little meat. To become almost a vegetarian.

Not be constipated, but above all never to take drastics such as Scamonee, Aloes, Jalap.

Take light infusions of Bourdaine or still better Paraffin oil.

194

Local Treatment

Use the canule to bring into the rectum a little *Sedosol*. In cases
of itchings rub gently with *Sedosol* and the soothing effect is felt
immediately.

Take great care before every application to make a good lotion
of hot boiled water.

Our product, which is a real new piece of science, does not
grease or stain the skin and is put away very easily even with
cold water.

Twice a day, therefore, they turned him over on his stomach and doctored his rectum. Between times they lubricated
his system so thoroughly and conscientiously that if he had
been a Linotype machine or a Diesel engine he would have
functioned smoothly for a year to come. But he was a trying
patient. Instead of being grateful to them for their pains he
yelled and cursed. He complained because the ice melted too
fast and grumbled when they refused to read to him. He
asked for *Jerusalem* by Pierre Loti and they brought back
Claude Farrere—*L'Homme Qui Assassina*. They were busy
again putting arms and legs together, dyeing wigs, making
hinges, sewing garments for their shooting gallery of Lillipu-
tians. All day long and far into the night they labored, and
while they labored they banged and scraped and whistled
and sang in Russian and French and German, and they tossed
off vodkas and gorged themselves with sandwiches, with
caviar and sturgeon. They removed the old bulbs which had
given out a yellow, sickly light and substituted daylight
lamps. The effect was shattering. It seemed to him as if his
flesh were a mass of splinters, that his nerves were exposed
and scraped. He could feel the veins in his rectum throbbing,

the blood bubbling there as if it were coursing through a wild pulse. And of what interest to him was their wild gibberish about Picasso and Rimbaud or the Comte de Lautréamont? They talked as if they were already seated on the *terrasse* in front of the Dôme. They even fixed the date of their going and disputed hotly as to which line they would take and whether they would live in a cheap hotel or rent a studio. They knew in advance that they would not be taking baths except at long intervals, that Camels would be too expensive to smoke, and that a sou wouldn't buy even a brass button.

How the piles alone are sufficient to make a man nervous and irritable; they weigh you down and make you feel as if your insides were dropping out. They can become so cursedly unbearable that the thought of hanging by the wrists becomes an unmitigated pleasure. But when, all day long, and far into the night, the place is turned into a carpenter shop and there is the sound of glasses clinking and tongues wagging, a man may be excused for going off his nut. And Tony Bring behaved exactly as if he had gone cuckoo. He yelled with pain or rage, and then he sang, and after that he cursed or laughed. If they mentioned Picasso he would talk about Matisse, or that wild man Czobel, and neither Czobel nor Matisse meant anything to him, nor did anybody, but he wanted to be heard and drown them with words, or if he couldn't drown them asphyxiate them because if they went on talking and talking he felt his guts would turn to sawdust and it would be the tale of the fake tinder fungus all over again. Injecting bisulfide of carbon or arsenate of lead wouldn't help a damned bit. A man who's being strangled in the rectum, who asks nothing more of the world than a saddle of cracked ice, can't be expected to have the temper of a saint or the heroism of a god. He wants to be left alone in peace and quiet, in a dark room preferably, and listen to some kind angel read aloud from some enchanting or disenchanting book. He doesn't want to hear of poems bordered by copper light or houses that open like oysters. He doesn't want to amuse himself with Chinese puzzles, for it was nothing less than a Chinese puzzle and would always remain one where Hildred had gone the night of the blizzard when she stepped out in a velvet suit with hollow silver balls down the front to mail a letter and then after not showing up for three days and nights neither telegraphing nor telephoning suddenly walks in with glassy eyes saying that she had met a poet and not even a punctuation mark beyond this. And if she thought everything could be put straight again by calling in a sawed-off, hammered-down runt of a doctor she was mistaken. He wouldn't have any cheap kikes tinkering with him, not even with his rectum. But the doctor came just the same and it was the old trick of slipping a thermometer under the tongue and asking questions you couldn't answer. A strange thing was that instead of talking about Capablanca or Einstein the doctor spoke of Hilaire Belloc, who he said was a scholar without wisdom, and anyway for the Gentile to deal with the Jews was like running a race with your legs tied because the Jewish mind was keen, quick, slippery, capable of turning over a thousand times to the Gentile's once. Hildred, who was greatly offended by her husband's rudeness, ushered the doctor to the front door and apologized, and the doctor kissed her hand and said there was nothing to worry about. "He's lazy . . . he's malingering," he said. And so with a light heart she returned to her carpenter shop and thereafter paid not the slightest heed to groans, aches, screams, curses, threats, laughs, et cetera.

Left to himself, ignored like a broken umbrella, the pain gradually easing up, because with time everything passes, Tony Bring discovered that it was pleasant to lie back and rehearse the drama of his life—a drama that began, as he vividly recalled, from that moment when, sitting in his high chair, he recited like a trained dog some verses of German poetry . . . recited in the barbarous tongue of his barbarous ancestors. So vivid, accurate, and complete were his recollections that with a fierce, proud, crazy exultation he said to himself: If I lie here long enough I can string my whole life together, day by day. And certain days which for certain reasons stood out from the others like milestones he did actually live over again, hour for hour, minute for minute. Women who had so completely dropped from memory that a week ago he could not have summoned their image now came to life in strictest detail—height, weight, resistance, texture of skin, the things they wore, the way they embraced . . . everything . . . everything. Retracing the curve of his life he saw that it was not the broad, circuitous arc that one imagined to himself, that it was neither an arrow shot toward death nor the parabolic kiss of the infinite nor yet the noble symphony of biology; it was rather a succession of shocks, a seismographic record of oscillations, of peaks and dips and broad, tranquil valleys that were like divine menopauses.

LATE ONE afternoon, as if electrified, he sprang out of bed, consumed a hearty meal in which he violated all the rules of diet that had been laid down for him, and began to write. The louder they banged, the more they whistled and guzzled and sang, the better he wrote. The words rose up inside him like tombstones and danced without feet; he piled them up like an acropolis of flesh, rained on them with vengeful hate until they dangled like corpses slung from a lamppost. The eyes of his words were guitars and they were laced with black laces, and he put crazy hats on his words and under their laps table legs and napkins. And he had his words copulate with one another to bring forth empires, scarabs, holy water, the lice of dreams and dream of wounds. He sat the words down and laced them to chair with their black laces and then he fell on them and lashed them, lashed them until the blood ran black and the eyes broke their veils. What he remembered of his life were the shocks, the seismographic orgasms that said, "Now you are living," "Now you are dying." And the broad tranquil valleys that were coveted was the cud which cows chewed, was the love which women took between their legs and masticated, was a bell with an enormous clapper that broke the wind with its clangor. The peaks and the dips—there was the living, the rush of mercury in the thermometer of the veins, the pulse without a bridle. The peaks—saint going up to peep at the hinderparts of God . . . prophet with dung in his hands and foaming at the mouth . . . dervish with music in the balls of his feet, with snakes squirming in his entrails, dancing, dancing, dancing with maggots in his brain. . . . Not heights and depths, but ecstasy upside down, inside out, the bottom reaching as far as the top. Abasement not reaching just to the earth, but through the earth, through grass and sod and subterranean stream, from zenith to nadir. Everything that was loved being hated fiercely. Not the cold pricks of conscience, not the tormenting flagellation of the

mind, but bright, cruel blades flashing, scorn, insult, con-
tumely, not doubting God but denying Him, flaying Him,
spitting on Him. *But always God!*

AND THEN one night Vanya rose up like a dolphin covered
with mud and she said, "I'll go mad . . . go mad!" and he said
to himself, Fine! Here we are at last . . . *go mad!* To go mad is
to stop being a eunuch, to quit the fertile valleys, not to
masturbate with paint or to change names. If she would only
go mad he would embrace her in madness, she male and he
female; he would put an infibulator on the house and they
would die of excess. And the amphibious one, who changed
sex with the seasons, who closed herself in like an oyster and
called the two hard shells her mystery, she could nurse her
mystery in iodine and mud. Colder than a statue, her voice
lifeless, her eyes glassy, the one who was mystery stood
beside the gut table. Like a sleepwalker stabbing herself over
and over. A dress rehearsal before an empty house, an im-
promptu debacle in which the actress revenges herself upon
the author. Wherever her feverish eyes turned there were
arms and legs and purple wigs, and lying in a corner like an
old mandolin was the Count and the Count had his ears
cocked, straining to catch the gurgle of the drains, the fall of
water falling, choked with ice and liquid fire and clots of
blood and violets that muttered. She was like a sleepwalker
stabbing herself over and over and out of the wounds that she
gouged with a broken knife her magnificent ego spilled forth
in sawdust gestures. Looking through the mist between her
eyes she saw mountains and vast alkali sinks and mesas dotted with sagebrush where at night the thermometer dropped
like an anchor and the wind moaned.

Big Vanya sat down and shut her ears so that everything might begin over again; she doubled up and went slack and her body rolled into a knot, her body legs and arms all snakes, a ball made of rubber bands. Immobile, breathing like a fetus, and if there were any thoughts in her they were drowned in her navel, if she had been asked her name she would not have known were it Miriam, Michael, David, Vanya, Esther, Ashteroth, Beelzebub, or Romanoff. So deeply, blindly, savagely did she crawl into herself that she was both womb and fetus and what moved and quivered in the beyond was like the thumping upon a swollen belly . . . thump, thump . . . a wild mare stamping on her belly, her croup curved like the arc of the sky.

With the statue standing there cold, eyes glassy, stabbing herself over and over, it was like a film in which the same shot is shot a hundred times. Every time the shutter clicked the eye plunged deeper into dream. Repetition death and the violence of death dream of living. Dream and death . . . the same shot shot a hundred times. With each click of the shutter the eye plunging deeper. Mute marble licked with eroticism, black ecstasy projected on screen-white fantasy. Hysteria. Hysteria of stone. Female stone shivering with music. Statue fornicating truth. Statue masturbating lies. Masturbation incessant, obscene . . . a rubber litany in a rubber dream. A hysterical woman with marble organs, a woman of marble with hysterical organs, a female stone spewing its guts is a fountain of fire breaking through ice. A hysterical woman may believe anything about herself—that she slept with Napoleon or offered her lips to God. She may say that she satisfied her appetite with goats or Shetland ponies, she may confess to loving six men at once and each of them with all her strength. She may shiver so with music that even the memory of her passions disintegrates, collapses like a burning building. Everything burns away that is not stone. The organs remain intact, mute marble licked with eroticism, ecstasy hung on a white screen. Lock all the doors and set the house on fire, where the statue stands masturbating lies there will still be music, the shiver of stone on fire, fire gushing through ice. Stab her over and over, plunge the eye deeper into dream, nothing but the repetition of death, eyes glassed with ecstasy, each click of the shutter a lie, a fornication. When women with marble organs essay to sleep with God, divinity arrives at menopause. What was ancient drama, noble music of myth and legend, ends in prophylaxis. Those who once felt themselves characters see their lines and gestures dribble away in sawdust. Once the world was young and the wounds one bore one displayed proudly, because God had put His finger in the wounds and they were not meant to heal—they were to be borne with courage and suffering. And now we are riding out like rotten sloops to the storm and you can poke an umbrella through the gaping holes of our wounds—but there is no suffering, and no courage. We and our characters—for we are our characters—go down like deserted ships, sloops too rotten to weather the first storm.

Finis.